"YOU'VE TURNED MY LIFE UPSIDE DOWN, SUE."

Jason continued huskily, "I'd resigned myself to the fact that a part of my life was over, then you came along and suddenly I'm experiencing the same basic drives of a man half my age." He paused, then put a hand to her cheek. "I'm not sure if you're the best thing that's ever happened to me...or the worst."

She smiled at him through a sudden blur of tears and covered his hand with hers. "Just give us a chance, Jase. That's all I ask."

He lowered his head and brushed his mouth against hers. "God, Sue...I think we'd better give ourselves some time to deal with all this."

And Susan knew that to hold him, she was going to have to let him go.

ABOUT THE AUTHOR

Calgary author Judith Duncan was born and raised in rural Alberta, and like the heroine in *All That Matters*, she harbors a deep love of the West. Her sixth Superromance is a sensitive, emotion-packed story that's destined to be read over and over again.

Books by Judith Duncan

HARLEQUIN SUPERROMANCE

Don't miss any of our special offers. Write to us at the following address for information on our newest releases.

Harlequin Reader Service
901 Fuhrmann Blvd., P.O. Box 1397, Buffalo, NY 14240
Canadian address: P.O. Box 603,
Fort Erie, Ont. L2A 5X3

Judith Duncan

ALL THAT MATTERS

Harlequin Books

TORONTO • NEW YORK • LONDON
AMSTERDAM • PARIS • SYDNEY • HAMBURG
STOCKHOLM • ATHENS • TOKYO • MILAN

Published March 1987

First printing January 1987

ISBN 0-373-70251-5

Printed in Canada

CHAPTER ONE

THE SENSE OF SPACE was almost overwhelming. For years, she'd heard her boss refer to it as "blue sky country," but she'd assumed it was just another catchphrase from the west, like "beautiful British Columbia" or "sunny Alberta." But this one was true. She'd never seen sky like this in her entire life.

Squinting against the glare of sunlight off the hood of her car, Susan Lynton's expression became thoughtful. This drive across Canada had certainly been an eye-opener for her. It was during the long journey that she finally realized what a narrow textbook concept she had of her native land. Having lived in Ontario all her life, Susan was fairly knowledgeable about the heavily populated and industrialized central part of Canada, but it wasn't until these past few days that she realized how little she knew about the rest of the country.

The forsaken wilderness of northern Ontario had filled her with a feeling of solitary awe. The miles and miles of forest was punctuated with craggy outcrops and countless crystal-clear lakes. There was a raw, wild beauty about it, but there was also a haunting aura of isolation. The silence of the uninhabited wilderness was eerie, almost smothering in its intensity, and Susan had never experienced such an overwhelming sense of loneliness.

The great plains of Manitoba and Saskatchewan had seemed like freedom, and the tabletop flatness and the sense of never-ending space had invigorated her until the monotony of the arrow-straight highway encased her in boredom. The towering grain elevators that crowded against the railroad in every town appeared like immobilized Goliaths, giants that dominated the fertile sweeping fields, subsisting on enormous quantities of grain. And she was intimidated by it all.

Now, as she traveled south from Calgary, the prairie plains heaved and buckled into the treeless bleak foothills of cattle country, and Susan experienced an uncomfortable feeling that she'd been royally conned. Her boss in Ottawa had inundated her with propaganda on the wonders of Alberta, thundering from his soapbox of enthusiasm, "It has everything, Susan—the prairies, the foothills, the mountains. It has wheat fields and forests. You travel Alberta, Susan, and you'll see for yourself. It's God's land." Susan grinned to herself. Clayton Chisholm was probably the most articulate salesman, the most fervent evangelist for the west in all of Ottawa.

Her smile faded as she adjusted her sunglasses, and a slight frown appeared. One of these days, though, she was going to regret her tendency to get swept into situations by other people's enthusiasm. And she had a nagging suspicion it was going to be much sooner than she expected.

When Clayton Chisholm had first suggested that she take an extended holiday from her very demanding job as his executive assistant, she had shrugged it off. But when he offered her a job on the ranch he and his nephew owned in the Alberta foothills, her interest had been sparked. Now that she was rapidly approaching her destination, she was beginning to wonder if her decision had been a wise one, especially when it had been so strongly colored by his enthusiasm, her own curiosity and an unfulfilled fantasy.

The curiosity was aroused by Clayton Chisholm himself. Even before she went to work for him seven years ago, Susan had been well aware of his impressive record as an elected member of Parliament. He had tirelessly served his southern Alberta constituency, and when his party, which had sat in opposition for many years, had enjoyed a sweeping victory in a recent federal election, he had been appointed minister of a very major portfolio.

Susan knew everything there was to know about his public life. But she knew very little about his private one. For all his affability, there was a certain reserve about the man. Many listed him among their most trusted and valued friends, but no one knew who was closest to Clayton Chisholm. Even though he had just turned sixty, he was still an Ottawa hostess's dream come true—a man who was eligible, successful and financially secure. He possessed a natural charm, an unquestionable masculinity, and it was no secret that the honorable member had more than one Ottawa socialite in determined pursuit. Over the years a multitude of idle, unfounded rumors had surfaced about his private life, but he'd never even bothered to acknowledge them. Clayton Chisholm's private life was exactly that: private.

No one had ever been allowed any personal glimpses. No one, except Susan.

It had happened six winters ago, shortly after she started to work for him as a junior researcher. A government scandal had been uncovered involving a senior party member who had been a colleague of Clayton's for many years. When accusations were shouted across the floor of the House of Commons that the honorable member, Clayton Chisholm, who held such an influential post in the opposition's shadow cabinet, had known what was going on, the public outcry was heard right across the country. The members of the governing party and the press gallery had a field day demanding his resignation. No one, except Susan, ever knew how close they came to getting it.

It had been right at the peak of the crisis, after days of unpleasant publicity and parliamentary mudslinging, that Susan saw a side of her boss that she intuitively knew no one in Ottawa had seen before. She had gone back to his offices at the parliament buildings one night to try to document a certain sequence of events that would clear his name. It had been very late and she was exhausted, but she'd continued to go through box after box of old files, looking for the information she needed.

She was seated at a table in Clayton Chisholm's office, cartons filled with thick file folders stacked around her, a nearly hopeless task ahead. The futility of what she was doing, combined with fatigue, finally wore her down, and in a fit of frustration, she'd thrown a file across the room, then buried her head in her arms and wept.

She hadn't heard him come into the office and wasn't even aware of his presence until he patted her reassuringly on the shoulder and commented wryly, "Don't despair, Susan. Nothing is ever so bad that it can't get worse."

The dryness in his tone struck her funny and she found her shoulders shaking with a mixture of tears and unexpected laughter. Wiping her face, she sat back in her chair and with a deep sigh, looked up at him. "Thanks a lot," she said, her tone as dry as his own. "I really needed to hear that."

His famous smile was a little ragged as he patted her shoulder again then went to his desk and wearily slouched into the chair behind it. "I'm beginning to think that anyone who gets involved in the machinations of bureaucracy is either the village idiot or totally insane."

Susan propped her chin on her hand, her previous sense of hopelessness giving way to amusement. "May I quote you on that?"

He laughed as he leaned back and laced his fingers behind his head. "The headhunters would wet themselves in utter delight if you did." His expression grew solemn as he stared off into space, his face lined with fatigue. After a moment of silence he turned his gaze to Susan. "Have you been able to nail down those dates?"

She shook her head, a defeated sag to her shoulders. "Not yet. I'm afraid it's going to take a while."

He pursed his lips and nodded, a frown furrowing his brow. Again he gazed off into space, then inhaling deeply, he leaned forward and rested his arms on top of his desk. He solemnly studied her for a second, then spoke, determination in his voice. "We're wasting our time. I've decided I'm going to hand in my resignation."

Susan couldn't have been caught more off guard, and she stared at him in disbelief. Finally she found her voice and stammered, "B-but you can't."

"Why not?"

The thought of his resigning left her speechless, and it took her a moment to gather her thoughts. "Because you know the allegations are unfounded, and given enough time, we can prove it."

He gave her a warped smile, and for the first time since she started working for him, Clayton Chisholm looked his age. "I'm not a young man anymore, my dear, and I'm getting tired."

She had found it impossible to meet his unwavering gaze, and she dropped her eyes and began to fiddle with the papers scattered before her. "I can understand that. But don't quit now. You have to see it through." He made no response but continued to stare at her. She had begun to think she'd overstepped her bounds, then she saw a tiny hint of humor gleaming in his eyes. She flashed him a smile and pushed the issue. "And besides, if you quit, I'll be out of a job."

He gave her an amused look as he tipped his head toward the boxes of files. "With that ahead of you, I'm surprised you still want it."

She'd left her chair and was kneeling on the floor, picking up the papers that had scattered from the file when she'd thrown it across the room. Tucking her hair behind her ear, Susan looked up at him and grinned. "Since I've started working, I've developed a habit of eating regularly and the novelty hasn't worn off yet.''

Clayton Chisholm chuckled and nodded.

There was more fact than fiction in that statement, Susan silently acknowledged as she stuffed old letters into the file folder. She had gone to work for him as soon as she'd graduated from university with a B.A. in public relations, and a regular paycheck had been heaven. But the real truth was that she absolutely loved her job.

She stuck the last sheet in the folder and stood up. A feeling of apprehension settled on her as she quietly studied him. He was hunched over his desk, a preoccupied expression on his face as he slowly rolled a pen between his fingers.

With her voice muted by uncertainty she asked, "Have you already tendered your resignation?''

The lines on his face seemed to be more deeply etched when he raised his head and looked at her. Without breaking the silence, he reached into the breast pocket of his jacket, withdrew a single folded piece of paper and handed it to her. Her spirits sank when she unfolded the heavy white bond and saw the familiar silver and blue insignia on the letterhead.

"I was on my way to hand deliver it, but I saw the light on in here.''

As she stood there staring at Clayton Chisholm's letter of resignation, the only coherent thought that surfaced was *I can't let him do this*. But when she finally looked at him, she saw him with clearer vision, her belief in his invincibility no longer distorting her view. The man was exhausted, both mentally and physically, and right then he looked old, very old—and very alone.

Her tone was gentle. "Will you hang on to this," she asked, indicating his letter, "and give me until the weekend to dig through this mess?"

"You may never find the documentation we need, you know," he responded, quietly preparing her for defeat.

"Yes, I will."

Clayton Chisholm watched her for the longest time, then said quietly, "I hope your father is damned proud of you."

A rueful smile appeared as she refolded his letter. "He wavers between pride and exasperation."

He responded with a snort of amusement and Susan looked at him. Her face sobered as she scrutinized his expression for some clue to what he was thinking. "Do I have until the weekend?"

He dragged his hand across his face and sighed. "Yes, you have until the weekend." He lowered his eyes and stared at his clasped hands, his face suddenly haggard.

She gazed at him, concern darkening her eyes. "What is it?" she asked softly.

There was a long silence, and when he finally spoke, his voice had a sad, reminiscent timbre to it. "There are times when I wonder why I've kept on going." There was something in his tone that made her realize there was a specific reason why he drove himself so hard, a reason why he had never married. And for Clayton Chisholm, it was a very private reason.

After that night, after gaining an unexpected insight into the man, Susan's compassion was aroused.

And when Susan's compassion was aroused, she mothered with unrelenting dedication. Instead of looking upon him as her boss, she began viewing him as a favorite uncle. Not only did she find the documents they needed to clear his name, she also uncovered some unexpected information that placed the integrity of Clayton's most vocal accuser on the line. Eventually the storm blew itself out, but from then on, Susan did everything she could to take the pressure off, to anticipate problems, to be one step ahead of his needs.

At first he had viewed her actions with a certain amount of amusement, but he began to depend on her more and more. In time, she became his confidante, and she was responsible for everything from approving his itinerary to editing his speeches to keeping him informed on even the smallest matter that might impact his department. An alliance of mutual trust and respect developed between them, and after working so closely together for so long, they'd reached a point where they could read each other perfectly.

They shared a solid rapport, and Susan knew she was closer to him than anyone else was in Ottawa, yet there was still that private part of his life she knew nothing about. She'd catch him in an unguarded moment, a haunted look in his eyes, an expression of such loneliness carved in his face that it would make her want to cry. The reason, she suspected, would be found here in the place he still considered home.

Susan's wandering thoughts were dragged back to the present when a white road sign with the wild rose emblem on it flashed past. She pulled onto the shoulder of the road and stopped, then extracted a road map from the narrow space between the emergency brake and the bucket seat. Pushing her sunglasses on top of her head, Susan refolded the map to isolate the last leg of her journey. Assured that this was the right turnoff, she slid the map back in the slot, replaced her glasses, and after checking for traffic turned west on the secondary highway.

The foothills rose before her, blocking out the distant panorama of the mountains. As she continued due west, she was surrounded by nothing but bleak, rolling hills. There was a quality of desolation about this part of the country that she hadn't expected. It seemed so barren, so empty, not at all how she had pictured it from Clayton's descriptions. Her doubts became even more unsettling. She didn't know if she could stand all this vastness, this *nothingness* for three months.

And she was, unfortunately, committed to three months. Clayton had arranged a two-month leave of absence for her while the house was in summer recess, and she had taken a month's holidays. But she was committed for other reasons. His sister-in-law had had a stretch of very poor health, and her doctor had warned that she had to take it easy for a while. Clayton was concerned that unless he stepped in, Mattie Chisholm would simply ignore doctor's orders and carry on. He felt that the summer work load was simply too much for a woman her age, and was convinced his executive assistant was the one and only candidate for the job.

He talked to Susan about hiring on as cook then let her think about it, and the longer she thought about it the more she wanted to go. Ever since she was a kid,

Susan had harbored a love affair with the west, and the idea of spending time on a working ranch held enormous appeal. So with her judgment colored by Clayton's enthusiasm, Susan took his word that the job would be a piece of cake.

Susan grinned to herself. Some cook. She could organize a banquet for four hundred without blinking an eye, but she was beginning to wonder if she'd be able to slap three big meals a day on the table for a crew of men. She had grown up on a tobacco farm in southwestern Ontario, which didn't really mean much under the circumstances, but a favorite uncle owned a large mixed farming operation in Manitoba, and until she started working during her high school years, Susan had spent a part of every summer vacation there. Even as a kid, who had more important things on her mind, like jumping out of the hayloft or chasing gophers, she was vaguely aware that her aunt spent most of her day preparing meals and doing dishes. Well, at least all those summer vacations would stand her in good stead now. She could tell one end of a cow from the other.

Suddenly, her few small doubts became very large ones. What did she *really* know about these people, anyway? Clayton often talked about his family and she felt as though she knew them, but actually they were still strangers. Susan knew from bits and pieces of conversation that Clayton's parents had been dead a long time, that his brother had been killed many years ago in a riding accident and that it was that brother's son who was now managing the ranch. She knew that the nephew's name was Jason, and that he was the father of four children who ranged in ages from thirteen to six. She knew he was divorced and in his middle forties, and she knew that his mother, who had done considerable traveling, had moved back to the ranch at the time of his divorce to help him raise the kids. And she also knew, with sudden absolute certainty, that she had made a very big mistake.

The narrow highway became more twisting and Susan blocked off her glum thoughts to focus her full attention on her driving. Cut into a steep bank, the road wound its way down into a deep ravine that had been carved by centuries of erosion. The drone of the engine changed pitch as Susan shifted into a lower gear while she navigated the sharp curve at the bottom of the gully. The sound of her passage echoed hollowly as she crossed a narrow wooden bridge that spanned a small stream, which lost itself in the random growth of wild berry bushes and stunted willows. A long incline zigzagged out of the ravine, and she geared down again when the engine protested the long, steep climb.

As she approached the crest of the hill, Susan experienced the same feeling she had from time to time when she was small: that she had reached the edge of the world and there was nothing on the other side.

But there was. And it was so breathtaking it was beyond description. She pulled over on the gravel shoulder and switched off the ignition, overwhelmed by the vista that was spread out before her. The ridge of bleak hills formed the natural rim of a valley that opened up to the most spectacular view she'd ever seen.

Off in the distance, the snowcapped Rocky Mountains loomed up in majestic splendor, creating an impregnable barrier that thrust jaggedly into the clear blue May sky, their imposing fortresses shaded in hues of blue, purple and gray. A high range of hills, densely covered by coniferous forest, rose against the base of the mountains and added a misty dimension of distance to the diorama. Here the range was no longer treeless, and coppices of poplar and aspen were scattered across the landscape, their crowns brushed with soft wisps of green from the first buds of spring. Sturdy sentinels of fir and spruce towered above the newly budding trees, their dark green boughs accentuated by the delicate shades of new growth.

The sky, blue and endless, encompassed it all. The colors were magnificent. From the purples, blues and grays of the mountains, to the variegated greens of the forests, to the rusts, ambers and golds of the rolling grassland—it was an artist's palette, and she absorbed every nuance of it.

Susan had no idea how long she sat there, entranced by the beauty before her, but when she finally stirred and reluctantly started the car, she felt as though she had just been given a long, cool drink after a very tiring journey.

Maybe she hadn't made a mistake, after all. The feeling of expectation grew as she covered the final miles, her host of doubts no longer badgering her. It was the strangest sensation, but she suddenly felt as if she were coming home.

And that feeling became even stronger as she crested a small rise and saw a group of buildings off to the right. It all seemed so familiar. "The buildings are set off to the north in a little hollow that's a fair distance from the main road," Clayton had told her when he gave her directions. "The first thing you'll see is a windbreak of spruce trees along the drive and the big white arena where Jason trains his horses. There's a typical ranch gate, a pole arch with the Double Diamond brand carved into the crossbar. You can't miss it.''

As Susan slowed to turn into the gate, she glanced up at the impressive row of gigantic spruce that lined the far side of the drive. Their roots went deep into this Chisholm land, as did Clayton's. Why, she wondered, did he ever leave, feeling the way he did about this place?

The lane curved down into a sheltered hollow, and Susan felt a rush of warmth as the house and buildings came clearly into view. Several acres of land adjacent to the road had been left untouched, and thick stands of poplar and pine were scattered across the rolling terrain. The driveway, which angled sharply across the yard, separated the raw untouched land from the lawn surrounding the Chisholm home.

The huge old-fashioned house, which faced the gravel driveway, looked like it had been recently painted, its black trim standing out sharply against the sparkling white. A veranda stretched across the front of the building, the still-bare branches of vines tangled profusely along the spindled rail and up the pillars at the corners.

A high hedge of lilacs, which was just beginning to show the first touch of spring, bordered the east side of the yard. Through the bare branches, Susan could see flashes of sunlight off the metal roof of the arena she had first seen from the road. Another windbreak of trees was located a fair distance behind the house, which, she suspected, hid the rest of the farm buildings and corrals from view. The setting was picture-book perfect.

She followed the driveway around to the back of the house where the road continued on, disappearing into the trees. Susan parked her aging Volkswagen beside a row of caraganas, and as she switched off the ignition, her uncertainties came marching back in full force. Taking off her sunglasses and hanging them on the sun visor, Susan combed her fingers through her shoulder-length, curly hair, then mentally squaring her shoulders, she climbed out of the car.

She was just passing through the broad opening in the hedge when the screen door opened and a woman with snow white hair came out. She was of medium height with a surprisingly good figure, and as she came down the steps, she brushed her navy slacks, which had smudges of flour across the front of them.

This was not exactly a grandma of the first order. Not the kind that spent her winter evenings knitting mitts or mending socks, Susan was willing to bet. This was a woman who liked to be where the action was, who liked to face new challenges. But her face had compassion and humor written into it with every line, and her blue eyes held a warmth and understanding put there by years of laughter. And as she came toward Susan, her face wrinkled with a huge smile as she stretched out her arms in a gesture of unaffected welcome. It was as though she'd known the younger woman all her life, and Susan felt suddenly very much at ease.

''You have to be Clayton's Susan,'' Mattie Chisholm said warmly as she clasped Susan in an enveloping hug. "He's told us so much about you, I think I'd know you anywhere."

Clayton Chisholm's sister-in-law released her and Susan, who was several inches taller, smiled down at the older woman. "I am. And you must be Mrs. Chisholm."

"Mattie, dear. Mattie," she corrected firmly. "Don't make me feel any older than I already do." A large tan-and-black curly haired dog, the obvious product of wildly indiscriminate breeding, came bounding around the house, his stubby tail wagging furiously. He rollicked around in front of Mattie in a delirium of excitement, and she pushed him aside as he jumped up against her. "Down, Dudley! Down," she commanded sternly. "Don't get so wrought up."

Susan's eyes lit up and she laughed. For some reason, his name seemed oddly appropriate. At the sound of her laughter, he stopped his bouncing and perked his ears in her direction. He inquisitively tipped his head to one side as he studied her with bright eyes, then pushed his head roughly against her thigh, blatantly begging for attention. Susan stopped to stroke his glossy coat. "Well, hello Dudley," she said as the dog crowded against her legs, wagging his tail so hard he looked as if he were hinged in the middle. "Aren't you gorgeous."

From behind her came a light jingling and the sound of shod hooves on gravel, then the unmistakable creak of a saddle. "Gorgeous is stretching it a bit, don't you think?"

Straightening up, Susan turned around. A man mounted on a magnificent horse was silhouetted against the sun, the blinding brilliance radiating behind him in a fiery corona. Feeling strangely breathless, she shrugged, her expression still animated. "That's a matter of opinion. I think he's wonderful."

"I suspect the feeling is mutual."

The tone of his voice flustered her and she groped for something to say. Mattie unwittingly came to her rescue. "This is my son, Jason. And Jason, this is Clayton's Susan."

There was a slight hesitation, then Jason Chisholm signaled his mount with a light touch of his heel, and the horse moved forward out of the masking brightness of the direct sunlight. The animal, who tossed his head with a nervous arrogance, was a mahogany bay Appaloosa stallion. Susan didn't know much about horses, but she *did* know enough to realize that this was a superb specimen of horseflesh. She glanced up at the rider and a strange flutter unfurled in her midriff. Jason Chisholm wasn't so bad, either.

With him astride the restless animal, it was hard to judge how tall he was, but everything else about him registered with startling clarity. This man literally radiated an aura of strength and masculinity. He was powerfully built with heavily muscled shoulders, but beneath his unquestionable virility, beneath his physical toughness, there was something . . . some indefinable quality that drew her. She wondered what kind of person *really* lay beneath the macho image.

And Jason Chisholm did have a macho image. He looked as if he had just ridden off a western set for a highly successful beer commercial. He was dressed in faded blue jeans and a dark blue plaid western-style shirt that fit him like a second skin. Threaded through the loops of his jeans was a wide hand-tooled belt that sported an engraved silver buckle, and on his feet he wore a pair of scuffed cowboy boots. His face was heavily shadowed by the broad brim of his gray Stetson, but even that couldn't conceal the strong jawline. He was, in every sense, a man's man.

It was Jason Chisholm who finally fragmented her thoughts. Resting one arm on the saddle horn, he leaned forward and extended his other hand toward her. "Welcome to the Double Diamond."

Susan felt vaguely suspended as she met his steady gaze. Placing her hand in his, she was bombarded by disturbing new impressions. Handsome? No, not exactly, but there was a compelling attractiveness about him, an attractiveness that was unfeigned and indestructible. His eyes were hazel, flecked with gold and amber, and the thick long lashes accentuated their hypnotic intensity. His dark bushy eyebrows were heavily sprinkled with white, and the stubble of beard along his jaw showed silver in the sun.

There was something very intriguing about his face, something that touched her in the most profound way. It revealed a depth of character, an inner strength, but it also revealed an imperviousness that had been carved by disillusionment. It was the face of a man who had forged on alone, a man whose sensuous mouth had been hardened by grim determination. And Susan felt an immediate affinity for him that she had never felt for another human being. Her keen awareness of him as a man had an immobilizing effect on her, and she was conscious of nothing except the warmth of his touch and his unwavering gaze.

"I just made a fresh pot of coffee," Mattie said, shattering the spell. "Why don't you take a break, Jason?"

Susan was unwilling to break physical contact with this man, and she reluctantly withdrew her hand from his grasp.

The change in him was immediate. It was as if some vital link had been broken, and his expression was suddenly shuttered as he scrutinized her. He stared at her a second longer, then glanced at his mother. "I can't right now. Duffy and I are heading over to the south pasture to cut out the yearlings from that herd." Shifting his weight in the saddle, he gathered the reins and cued the stallion with a barely perceptible movement. As the horse and rider turned, Jason glanced down at Susan and touched the brim of his hat in a gesture that was as old and as traditional as the west itself. "Hope you enjoy your stay here," he said stiffly.

It was obvious that he had, for some reason, withdrawn behind a wall of cool politeness, and that bothered Susan more than she liked to admit. Her voice was uneven when she responded, "Thank you. I'm sure I will."

Their eyes connected, and for a split second his guard was down, and Susan experienced a sudden galvanizing rush that set her heart hammering wildly against her ribs. But beneath that electric undercurrent of sexual chemistry there was another, less pleasant feeling. Whatever initial attraction there was between them, it would go no farther. Jason Chisholm would see to that. He gave her another salute, and with an undetected signal the powerful bay snorted and arched his neck, then pivoted on his hind legs, fighting the restraint of the rider. But the rider's discipline was relentless. No one—not man or beast—would ever breach this man's control.

CHAPTER TWO

"THAT MAN WORRIES ME," Mattie said, an anxious frown appearing as she watched horse and rider disappear into the trees.

Susan glanced down at her companion. "Why?"

Mattie sighed and shook her head. "He drives himself too hard. If it wasn't for his horses, Jason would have absolutely nothing for himself."

"Clayton says he breeds championship quarter horses."

"He does, and he loves it. But he has so little time for it." She turned to face Susan and sighed, then gave her a wry smile. "Forgive me, Susan. You didn't come all the way out here to listen to me froth off about my son." She patted the younger woman's arm then motioned toward the house. "Come in. We'll have a coffee, then I'll show you around."

Susan studied her as they walked up the worn path, silently marveling at the snowy whiteness and thickness of the woman's wavy hair. But as they stepped into the harsh sunlight, Susan could see signs of poor health. Mattie's breathing was labored and her pulse, which was plainly visible in her neck, was very rapid. She looked utterly exhausted.

They climbed the steps and as Mattie opened the screen door, Susan caught the distinctive fragrance of cinnamon and lavender, and suddenly she felt homesick for her own grandmother—maybe *all* grandmothers smelled of cinnamon and lavender.

The porch was part of a large addition that had been built onto the entire back of the house. From it, doorways led to the left and to the right, the one on the right obviously leading into the main house.

Mattie indicated the space with a wave of her hand. "We added this part about thirty years ago. We needed a kitchen for the men and some sort of living quarters for the cook, when we had one." She pointed toward the door on the left. "I'll take you on a quick tour to show you your room."

Susan followed her, absorbing every detail as they entered the enormous kitchen. There was a large U-shaped work area with fairly new white Arborite-covered cupboards. Above the sinks, there was a large window facing west, offering a spectacular view of the mountains and foothills, and Susan mentally acknowledged that no job could possibly be tedious with a view like that.

Adjacent to the work area was the eating area, which was furnished with a massive table that would easily seat a dozen people. Along the north side of the kitchen there were four more windows that overlooked the backyard and the windbreak of trees beyond.

Although the walls could do with a fresh coat of paint and the whole place looked as though it could stand a thorough scrubbing, the room had a certain homeyness about it that Susan found very appealing. All the woodwork around the windows and doors was oak, the color darkened to a deep mahogany shade by repeated varnishings. The window ledges were wide and old-fashioned and held several pots of flourishing red geraniums. The floor was covered with old red and gray inlaid tile that showed faint trails of wear and spatterings of paint. None of the wooden chairs around the huge solidly built table matched, and the stove, which was enormous, looked like an old converted wood burner.

"Your room's in here," Mattie said as she led Susan around a corner to a short hallway that had two doors on either side and another door at the far end. The door on the right led into a small bathroom that housed a big old tub with clawed feet, and even from the doorway, Susan could detect the weird, wavy flaw in the mirror that covered the ancient medicine chest.

The door to the left led into a spacious bed-sitting-room. And stepping into it was like stepping back in time. The furniture was old and a little worn, but that didn't detract from the ageless beauty of it. Susan ran her hand appreciatively over the rich wood of the massive burl walnut dresser, which was still graced by the original beveled mirror set into a hand-carved frame.

The bed was metal, its most recent coat of paint being white. It was a marvelous old filigreed thing with a wild variety of curlicues, doodads and baubles twisted and turned into the elaborate design. It was amply covered by a handmade patchwork quilt of various prints and ginghams. The once-intense colors had faded with age and countless washings, but the intricate design was still distinct.

There were two well-worn armchairs, which were upholstered in a deep maroon embossed velour, standing on either side of an old lamp table that was, Susan was sure, made out of solid cherry wood. Two colorful hand-braided rag rugs lay on the dark wood floor, one beside the bed and one covering the floor beneath the two chairs. The three long narrow windows on the far wall were covered by old-fashioned fringed blinds and lace curtains. And in Susan's eyes, even with the signs of age and wear, this room was perfect.

"It's all a little old-fashioned, I'm afraid," Mattie said. "But on a ranch, new furniture is never a priority."

Susan grinned knowingly. "You can't convince me that you'd ever part with a single piece of this gorgeous old furniture."

Mattie shrugged, her smile a little sheepish. "Well, no I wouldn't, but sometimes young people don't understand that."

"Well, I certainly do. I'll enjoy every minute I spend in this room, believe me."

"I hope so." She smiled warmly at Susan and motioned toward the door. "Now I'm sure you're more than ready for that coffee."

Having left the bedroom, Susan turned to leave the way they'd come, but Mattie pointed toward the door to the left. "No, we can go into the main house this way. This door was here when we added on, so we just left it."

She opened it and entered another short hall. Again, there was a bathroom on the right and another door on the left, which was closed. Mattie motioned to it. "This is Jason's room. When I came to live with him, he insisted I move back upstairs into the master bedroom. It has a smaller room off it that used to be a nursery, so he fixed it up as a little sitting room. He thought that I might need a quiet place of my own now and again.''

Susan only caught a glimpse of the enormous living room as she turned and followed Mattie down another wide corridor toward the other smaller kitchen, but it was enough to comprehend just how large the Chisholm home was.

The rooms had high ceilings, which added to the spaciousness, but in spite of the size, there was still a special charm and warmth about the place that only came with age. Instead of being heavy and oppressive, the extensive ornate woodwork gave each room an air of durability and quality, and the beautiful antique furniture, which had obviously been in the Chisholm family for decades, reinforced the sense of solidness, of permanence, of unbroken continuation. It would be a very secure place to grow up in, Susan reflected, knowing that generations had gone before and generations would probably follow. She thought of the man with the steady hazel eyes, who was the product of those many generations. Perhaps that's why he was so solemn—the weight of that responsibility would not sit lightly on his shoulders.

The timer on the oven pinged, and picking up a pair of pot holders that were lying on the counter, Mattie opened the oven door. The mouth-watering aroma of hot cinnamon buns came wafting out, and Susan's empty stomach responded.

"I hope you aren't one of those women who's constantly dieting," Mattie said as she slid the cookie sheet onto a rack on the counter.

Susan laughed and shook her head. "Not me, Mattie. I tried it once and hated it."

"I'm glad to hear it. I'm afraid this preoccupation with thinness is not doing the younger generation much good."

Using tongs, Mattie broke off four of the enormous rolls and put them in a basket, then brought them to the table. They looked and smelled delicious, and Susan eyed them with relish as the older woman bustled around getting coffee, napkins and the cream and sugar.

Placing a side plate in front of Susan, Mattie glanced at the clock above the cupboards. "We made it just in time. The children will be home from school soon and if we hadn't already had ours by the time they get here, we'd be lucky to get even a nibble."

Slowly stirring the cream into her coffee, Susan smiled with fond recollection. "I can remember when we were kids how we'd tear home on the days Mom baked. I don't know why it was, but there was always something very reassuring and comforting about the smell of freshly baked peanut butter cookies when you'd had a lousy day."

Mattie smiled and nodded her head in agreement. "I know. That's exactly why I still do it."

Once again Susan was struck by how totally drained this woman looked, and she was trying to think of some tactful way of asking about Mattie's health when the older woman spoke. "You have brothers and sisters, Susan?"

Susan grimaced. "I most certainly do. There are seven of us—five boys and two girls."

"Goodness—seven! Were you the eldest?"

"No, I have two older brothers." She grinned and shook her head. "Looking back, I honestly don't know how Mom and Dad survived. We were such a bunch of little hellions."

A look of relief crossed Mattie's face. "I'm so glad you're used to children. These four can be a handful at times, and I was worried they'd bother you."

"They won't bother me, Mattie," Susan said reassuringly. "Kids and I usually get along pretty well."

Mattie studied the younger woman for a moment, then tipped her head and smiled, an astute gleam in her eyes. "Yes, I'm sure you do. I suspect there aren't many you can't handle."

Susan laughed. "Well, no, not many. But let's face it, I've had my share of practice."

"Well, I can assure you these four will give you some more. Patricia and Lucy aren't too bad, but those two boys are a handful." A look of weariness crossed her face. "There are times when they wear me right out."

That was apparent. After glancing around, Susan could see that *everything* was wearing her out. The rooms were tidy but there were signs everywhere that the house was simply too big for Mattie to handle: the windows needed to be washed, the kitchen floor desperately needed a scrubbing, and dust and fingerprints covered the furniture.

Coming from such a large family, Susan knew how much work was involved. But she had been raised in a home where the chores were shared, and even the boys had to help with housework. She had a sneaking hunch that was not the case here. Which meant that either Mattie was simply too tired to organize household tasks, or these kids were also a bunch of little hellions.

Susan found out a short time later about the Chisholm children. The two boys came boiling in the back door like dual tornadoes with jean jackets, lunch kits and school papers caught up in their momentum.

The first tornado turned into a stationary bundle of energy who was, unquestionably, all boy. He greeted his grandmother with open affection. "Hi, Grandma! Watcha making? Hey, cinnamon buns!" He turned and looked at Susan with unveiled curiosity. "Are you gonna be our new cook?"

There was an undertone of amusement in her voice as she nodded. "Yes, I am."

Mattie came forward and ruffled his hair affectionately. "This is Michael. He just turned ten." She smiled at the other boy who'd come to stand beside her. "And this is Todd. He's eleven and a half."

Todd met her eyes with the same steady hazel gaze as his father's, then flashed her a smile that was pure charm. "Uncle Clayton sure can pick 'em," he said, his grin deepening to reveal a big dimple in his left cheek.

Mattie gave him a stern look and opened her mouth to scold him, but Susan intervened. "You're much too young to be a flirt," she said, somehow managing not to laugh.

There was a contrived innocence about him that hinted of irrepressible mischief when he answered gravely, "Just covering my bases, ma'am."

Susan knew by the gleam in his eyes that she was faced with an inveterate tease, and she fell in love with the kid right there and then. "Covering your bases is one thing, Mr. Chisholm, but just don't try stealing any!''

Her response sent him into a fit of laughter, and she watched as he doubled over. A movement at the door caught her eye and she glanced over.

Two girls had entered and were standing in the doorway. The older one, who Susan knew was thirteen, was firmly holding the smaller girl's hand as she gravely watched her brother's performance. She wore her long, curly hair pulled back in a ponytail, the style accentuating her solemn eyes. *There,* thought Susan with sudden circumspection, *is a desperately unhappy child.* Seeing the girl brought back some not-so-happy memories of her own. She had gone through a period of a year or so when she had been really chubby, and she had hated every pound. Fortunately it was a stage she had eventually outgrown.

This girl, she suspected, would not be so lucky. The conversation with Mattie about dieting came to mind, and she had a feeling that this child was the reason for the woman's concern. Susan smiled at the girl who shyly smiled back, and she experienced a rush of sympathy. Adolescence could be such a rotten, lonely period, and from the expression in this girl's eyes, Susan guessed she was having a more difficult time than most.

The younger one was a different ball of wax altogether. She was all cute and bubbly and had a dimpled smile that would turn granite to mush. Her red-and-white dress was liberally trimmed with ruffles and lace, and there was a big red bow tied in her tumble of dark curls. She looked as if she had just tap-danced her way out of a Shirley Temple movie. She was a doll, and Susan suspected that this little Miss Chisholm certainly knew it.

"This is Patricia," Mattie said, indicating the older girl. "And this is Lucy," she added as she smoothed down the little one's curls. "Girls, this is Susan Lynton."

Both girls smiled their welcome, then went over to the counter and laid down the things they were carrying. For a moment, all four Chisholm children were grouped together, and Susan couldn't help but notice the strong resemblance Todd, Patricia and Lucy shared with their father. They had the same almond-shaped hazel eyes, the same straight nose, the same full mouth, and even though Jason hadn't smiled, she'd bet the farm he had a big dimple in his left cheek.

All four of them had brown curly hair, but Michael's was several shades lighter and had deep auburn highlights. It was, in fact, practically identical to Susan's. There was no question that the children were brothers and sisters, but Michael did not possess the unquestionable Chisholm likeness. She studied the boy a little closer and wondered why he seemed to be strangely familiar.

Just then, Michael lifted his head and looked directly at her. Susan experienced an eerie start of recognition, and an odd sensation fluttered in her stomach when she realized it was more than the same hair coloring they shared. Susan's eyes were an unusual shade of deep blue—delphinium blue, her grandfather used to say—and Michael's were the exact same shade. His wide eyes and dark arched brows dominated his oval face, and thick sweeping lashes accentuated his slanted cheekbones. His resemblance to her was so strong, so definite, he could have easily been her son.

A funny feeling unfolded in her that she tried to ignore. It was her maternal instinct rearing its head again, and that always got her into some sort of trouble. Susan smiled as she watched him worm a second cinnamon bun out of his grandmother; he might not have the Chisholm looks, but he certainly had the Chisholm charm.

THE NEXT TWO DAYS were fairly hectic for Susan, but once she found out where everything was, and was able to arrange a tenuous truce with the monstrosity of a stove, she settled into a comfortable routine. Except for suppers, she usually just had the four men to feed. There were the two hired hands, Duffy and Len, who lived in the big bunkhouse behind the garage, and Walter, a cousin of Clayton's, who had his own small house back in the trees. He'd been away helping a neighbor, and so far had only been home for two meals. And there was Jason.

She came to the conclusion that her first impression of him had been a figment of her imagination. He was not as he seemed; he was remote and abrupt, and after she'd been around him for a while, she could not for the life of her figure out why he had affected her so strongly.

By the fourth day, Susan had everything under control and was beginning to find time heavy on her hands. She liked being busy, but there wasn't really that much to do, and the boredom was starting to get to her.

As soon as the men left after dinner, she started eyeing the kitchen floor. It was a mess. It had such a thick buildup of wax some of it had to be ten years old. There were also spatters from previous paint jobs in a rainbow of colors, and there were so many black scuff marks that it looked like an entire army had marched through. She really couldn't stand to live with *that* for three months.

Rummaging around in the huge closet in the porch, Susan discovered a gallon can of Varsol and a very old floor polisher. When she had cleaned out the cupboard under the sink, she had found two full cans of liquid wax, so she had all she needed to do a thorough job. And really, what was the harm, she rationalized as she stacked the chairs on top of the table, especially when she'd be done in plenty of time to fix supper.

In less than an hour, she had nearly half the huge area stripped. It was going much faster than she expected, and the results were certainly amazing. Susan hummed to herself, feeling smugly satisfied with her efforts. She honestly didn't mind housework when she could see the results of her labor, and she could certainly see what she was accomplishing here.

She was using the floor polisher to scrub off the dissolved wax and the howl from the motor masked all other sounds. She did not hear the back door slam. What she did hear was somebody swear, and she whirled around just as Jason yanked the plug out of the wall. "What's going on here?" he demanded curtly.

He'd caught her so by surprise that all she could do was stand there and stare at him with her mouth hanging open. His curly salt-and-pepper hair was clinging damply to his temples, and he looked hot and cranky. He stared at her stonily. "You were hired to do the cooking. That's all. Nothing more."

Susan couldn't really see what the problem was, but his attitude was beginning to ruffle her feathers. It was almost as though he resented her being there, and that nettled her; it wasn't as if she was falling down on the job. But in spite of her annoyance, she managed to keep her voice relaxed as she answered, "I didn't have anything else to do so I thought I'd clean the floor."

"That is not what you were hired to do," he snapped, his chin stuck out a mile.

Okay, Susan, she inwardly steamed, *you won't lose your temper.* Aloud she said, "I realize that, but it needs to be done and I don't mind—"

"This is not your job," he retorted stubbornly.

Susan was beginning to see red, and she placed her hands on her hips, her own chin taking on a tenacious set. "This is totally ridiculous. While we're standing here arguing over whether I should or should not scrub the damned floor, the solvent is probably dissolving the glue." She stomped over and picked up the cord and under her breath, she muttered, "And I'll do as I damned well please."

The expression on his face was thunderous, but she ignored it and reached past him to plug the floor polisher back in. His arm shot out and he roughly caught her wrist and twisted her hand over. The skin, irritated by the harsh solvent, was red and slightly abraded, and Susan had the feeling he was just itching to give her supreme hell.

Just then, Duffy stuck his head in the door. "We've got the horses loaded and we're ready to roll, Jase."

Jason dropped her hand and glared at her, then he turned, and giving Duffy a slicing look, slammed his hat on his head and strode out the door. Duffy raised his eyebrows in a baffled expression but Susan only shrugged, feeling more than a little baffled herself. It didn't make much sense. He was acting as though he'd caught her starving the kids, instead of doing a monotonous household chore that most men didn't even know existed.

For the remainder of the afternoon, Susan alternated between a slow burn and a teeth-clenching vexation. She had the distinct feeling she'd been unjustly castigated simply because, as her grandmother would put it, "he felt like kicking the dog." Consequently, her mood bounced through everything from anger to feeling hard done by, but eventually a niggling little feeling wormed its way into her indignation. She had a tough time acknowledging it, but she finally had to admit that she was beginning to feel like an idiot for reacting the way she had.

Once she went that far, she also had to admit that her female ego had suffered a bruising the past few days, thanks to Jason's aloofness, and it was further bruised when he had jumped on her that afternoon. And somewhere between waxing the floor and washing the windows, it dawned on her that maybe Jason had never wanted her there in the first place, that maybe Clayton had rammed her down his throat. The more she thought about it, the more troubled she became, and the more troubled she became, the more she immersed herself in hard work. By the time five o'clock rolled around, she had cleaned every square inch of the kitchen and anything that could be scoured, scrubbed, waxed or polished had been. But as she surveyed the results of her efforts, she didn't feel the usual satisfaction from a job well done. Instead, she felt oddly discouraged.

After trying to shed her gray mood in a long hot shower, Susan put on a bright pink blouse that tied at the midriff, glumly hoping that the vivid color would pick up her spirits. Slipping into a new pair of blue jeans, she felt some satisfaction. For once, the length was adequate. She was tall, nearly five foot eleven, and it was nearly impossible to buy anything that was long enough in the legs. She had discovered at a very early age that if she wanted something decent to wear, she was going to have to make it herself. She smiled as she retied the blouse. Clayton had always kidded her that the only reason he hired her was because she was a "snappy" dresser and had enough class not to eat with her feet.

She put on a pair of leather thongs, then went out to the kitchen and got the vegetables she was going to prepare for supper out of the fridge. Filling the sink, Susan immersed a head of cauliflower and bunch of broccoli in the ice-cold water and grimaced when the wetness stung her raw, chapped hands.

As she reached for a paring knife, she glanced out the window. Lucy was standing on the rope swing that hung from a thick branch of an enormous poplar, pumping away as she sang at the top of her voice, her face contorting with outrageously affected expressions. She was obviously lost in some world of her own, and Susan grinned as she watched her. If this kid didn't end up an actress, there was no justice in the world.

Susan finished the vegetables and put them on the stove to steam, then started fixing the salad. Michael and Todd came around the garage with their ball gloves, a bat and a baseball. There was a loud argument about who would do what: Michael wanted to pitch to Todd, Todd wanted to bat flies for Michael to catch, and the whole time they argued, Dudley romped back and forth between them, wagging his tail in anticipation.

Susan stopped working, and bracing her hip against the counter, stuck her hands in the back pockets of her jeans. She'd quickly discovered that the Chisholm boys loved baseball. But then, so did she. The brother who was a year younger than she pitched for a major-league team, and while they were growing up, Susan was always the one Peter either conned or bullied into catching for him. Over the years, she had become somewhat of a pitching expert—and a damned good catcher.

Michael won the argument, and Todd moved back and crouched in a catcher's squat. With a knowing eye, Susan watched his windup and delivery. The pitch was high and outside, but for a boy his size, he had tremendous speed. She narrowed her eyes contemplatively as she watched him, but the vegetables boiled over and she was forced to turn her attention to the stove.

Supper, which was always at six sharp, turned out to be a strained affair. When the two boys came in to wash up they were unusually subdued, and Susan gathered by the murmured comments that they'd caught hell from their father for horsing around in the barn when they were supposed to be helping with chores. Lucy was sitting at her place at the table swinging her feet, animatedly engrossed in a whispered conversation with some imaginary friends, while Patricia sat cross-legged on another chair, her nose buried in a book.

When Susan heard the back door slam and masculine voices in the porch, she started carrying the steaming serving dishes to the table. Setting the basket of fresh buns at one end, she glanced at Patricia. "Tricia, would you please go tell your grandmother supper's ready?"

"Sure, Susan." Marking her place, she closed the book, laid it on a window ledge and left the room. Feeling very uncomfortable about their earlier clash of wills, Susan deliberately avoided looking at Jase as the men came in and sat down. She suspected that there wasn't much he missed, and it would only take a quick glance to see that not only had she defied him and finished the floor, but she had done considerably more. And she really didn't want another confrontation, especially in front of a bunch of people.

She put the last of the food on the table and had just taken her place when Patricia returned. "Grandma says she won't be in for supper, Susan. She's not feeling well."

Something made Susan glance at Jase, and she experienced a twinge of guilt when she saw how tired he looked. Dragging her attention away from him, she helped Lucy fill her plate. She'd slip in to check on Mattie later, she decided silently, and make sure there was nothing seriously wrong.

"I checked that south pasture today, Jase," said Duffy as he reached for a bun. "If we don't get some rain pretty soon, we're going to have to move that herd. Them cows have damn near grazed that grass down to dirt, and that creek'll be bone dry in a week."

Len nodded in agreement. "It's bad, that's a fact. I was talking to Cliff Seward yesterday. He says he's going to have to start culling his herd if he don't get a soaking pretty soon. Course, he was already in pretty bad shape last fall."

Susan poured some gravy on Lucy's potatoes, then looked at Len. "I thought most of the streams around here were mountain fed."

"Well, ma'am, they are. But we had a light snowfall last year and we just ain't had the runoff we usually get. There wasn't even that much snow in the mountains so them streams are pretty scant."

"We had a real dry summer and fall last year," explained Duffy. "So that ground's bone dry. It ain't going to grow nothin' but thistles. I doubt if there's a green blade of grass within a hundred miles, and you can't keep a herd alive on wishful thinkin'."

Susan digested that. No wonder Jason was so quick to fly off the handle when he was faced with a major drought. And her right-minded conscience piled more guilt upon her head. Okay, she'd apologize the first chance she got. *You'd better make it good,* niggled her conscience, *since he likely didn't want you here in the first place.* Wonderful. Now she really felt lousy.

"Hey, Dad, we have a baseball game in town tomorrow night. We play that High River team that beat us before." Todd put some dressing on his salad, then looked at his father. "I told Mr. Wilson you'd help, okay? He said he needed a base coach."

"What time?" They were the first words Jason had spoken since he'd come in, and the weariness in his voice made Susan inwardly wince.

"Six-thirty. Mikey's going to be the starting pitcher and Mr. Wilson's moving me to shortstop."

Jason rested his arms on the table and gazed at his eldest son. "Todd, I'd really like to help, but I likely won't make it back until after seven."

Michael broke in. "You mean you won't even be there to watch? It's going to be the first time I get to pitch, Dad, and you aren't even going to be there?" His voice rose sharply, and it was very apparent that he was upset. Susan could understand how he felt. His big chance to prove himself, and it was only natural that he wanted his dad there. But Susan could tell by the look in Jason Chisholm's eyes that the very last thing he needed today was this.

"You've never missed a game before," Todd said accusingly.

There was a strained silence as Todd and Michael fastened their eyes on their father. Susan had been a kid once; she knew exactly what they were trying to do. Only she wasn't going to let them get away with it. "I'll be a base coach for your team, Todd."

That got a response from the boys, and they stared at her as if she'd just waded through the mashed potatoes. "What do *you* know about baseball?" Todd said in a tone that was as close to a sneer as he dared in front of his father.

She stared right back. "I know enough to tell you that you miss most grounders that come at you from the right side, that you hardly ever miss a line drive and that you can really connect with a pitch that's a little high and outside." She gave him a superior smile then looked at Michael. "I know that you have a good fast ball, but you have a tendency to lose control when you throw sliders, which you shouldn't be throwing in the first place. And I strongly suspect that you like to steal bases."

There was another silence as they stared at her with dumbfounded looks on their faces. Susan managed to keep her face expressionless as she let everything sink into their devious little minds. Her facade of indifference was nearly shot to pieces when she glanced up and found Jase watching her. He had leaned back in his chair and was absently stroking his bottom lip with his thumb. There was a glint of amusement in his eyes and a hint of a smile around his mouth. As her gaze locked with his, Susan felt a warm flush color her cheeks, and she quickly looked away. She'd have given anything to know what was going through his mind right then.

"How do you *know* all that?" Michael finally stammered, his eyes still wide with amazement.

"Do you know Peter Lynton?"

"You mean the pitcher for the Blue Jays?"

Susan nodded. "I used to catch for him."

Michael's eyes looked as if they were going to pop right out of his head. "You *know* Pete Lynton?"

"He's my brother."

"Brother! Your brother!" If there was such a thing as seventh heaven, Michael had found it and he was squirming in his chair in an orgy of ecstasy. "Can you get me his autograph? Can you, Susan? I'd do anything to get his autograph! Just tell me what I have to do to get his autograph!''

"How about shoveling a trail through your room?" she responded dryly.

Jason cleared his throat, and Susan shot a quick look at him. For a split second she thought he was going to laugh, but he kept a straight face.

Patricia had been around baseball-crazy brothers long enough to know who Pete Lynton was. "Did you really catch for him?" she asked, her tone nearly as disbelieving as her brothers'.

"I did, and sprained every finger on both hands doing it." Realizing she'd managed to temporarily derail the two boys, Susan told them a bit about Peter and his career, deliberately steering Michael and Todd away from the topic of their upcoming baseball game. With a bit of luck she managed to get through the rest of the meal without giving them the chance to think about it.

The children remained at the table after the men left, indulging themselves in second helpings of Susan's rice pudding. Lucy was once again immersed in some imaginary drama, and Patricia had gone to see if her grandmother wanted anything to eat. For all intents and purposes Susan had the boys on their own. She knew that she was, as her grandmother would say, "sticking her oar in" where she had no business sticking it in, but she felt duty bound to say something.

Standing at the counter, she placed the leftover buns in a plastic bag before turning to face the boys. "Your dad has a lot on his mind right now, guys. And I don't think you were being very fair about your baseball game," she said quietly. Michael and Todd exchanged a quick glance, then as if caught in a conspiracy, they abruptly fixed their eyes on the table. But they did have the decency to look a little shamefaced as they suddenly became engrossed in cleaning every bit of pudding out of their dishes.

Susan went back to the table and started stacking dirty plates. "I don't think he'd miss one of your games unless he had to. You made him feel really bad about it, you know."

Todd shrugged uncomfortably. "Yeah, I know, but we like him to come."

"I know you do, Todd. All kids like their parents to go to things like that. But do you really think it was fair of you guys to lay a guilt trip on him the one time he can't?"

There was a short silence before Todd finally mumbled remorsefully, "No, I guess it wasn't." He looked at Susan and made a grimace of regret. "We didn't mean to make him feel bad. We were just trying—"

"Trying to apply enough pressure to get him to give in," she said with a lopsided smile. "I know. I was a kid once."

"Will you really come to our game, Susan?" Michael asked hopefully.

"Sure. I'd love to."

"And will you really help me with my pitching?"

"I will when I have time." Resting her hands on her hips, she gave them her best no-nonsense look. "Now, have either of you got homework tonight?"

"Yeah," they said in woeful unison.

"Well, you'd better get at it, okay?"

With a total lack of enthusiasm, they groaned as they slowly got up from the table and started dragging reluctant feet toward the door. As the boys disappeared onto the porch, she turned and lifted Lucy off the chair then set her down on her feet. "Would you go see where Patricia is, please? I need to know what Grandma would like for supper before I put everything away."

"What Grandma wants for supper," Lucy parroted as she skipped out of the room. Susan picked up the stack of dishes and turned toward the cupboards. She nearly dropped the whole pile when somebody spoke behind her.

"Mattie's asleep so I told Tricia not to wake her."

Her heart was pounding wildly and her hands weren't quite steady as Susan set the dishes down. She turned to face the unexpected visitor, who was standing in the doorway of the hall leading to the other entrance. His shoulder was braced against the doorframe, and Jase had his thumbs hooked in the pockets of his faded jeans, the stance pulling the fabric of his plaid shirt tautly across his chest. As he shifted his weight slightly, his altered position accentuated the strong contours of his jaw and the muscled thickness of his neck, and Susan was suddenly keenly aware of his powerful build.

In the diffused light from the hall, his hair had the same sheen as polished pewter, the silver shade contrasting sharply with his weathered tan and the dark fabric of his shirt. He was watching her with an intentness that Susan found unsettling, making her even more conscious of him as a man. Everything about him was disturbingly masculine: his looks, his size, his strength, even the way he moved. He possessed the same animal grace, the same energy as the magnificent stallion he rode, only Jase Chisholm's sexuality was rigidly contained behind a wall of cool reserve. And Susan found herself wondering what would happen if that wall was ever breached.

That line of suggestive thinking got her into deep and dangerous waters as vivid images took shape in her mind, and Susan suddenly found it difficult to breathe. The sensation intensified as Jase straightened and with the characteristic loose-hipped gait of a horseman, sauntered toward her.

There was something in his eyes, some vague expression touching on gratitude that was a dead giveaway, and Susan knew he had overheard what she had said to Michael and Todd. She prayed he wouldn't bring it up.

He didn't. Instead he recycled something that was nearly as awkward. "I owe you an apology for this afternoon," he said quietly.

She raised her shoulders in a gesture of embarrassment as she responded, "Couldn't we just forget it?"

Jase was standing very close to her, and Susan was transfixed by the intensity of his gaze as he shook his head. "No, we can't. I have a low boiling point at the best of times, but I had no right to jump you the way I did."

Something was happening between them that Susan couldn't quite define, but whatever it was, it was something she did not want to jeopardize. Her voice was oddly husky when she said, "My boiling point isn't much higher than yours. We're bound to strike sparks off each other."

The tiny lines around his eyes crinkled as he nearly smiled, and Susan felt her knees go weak. She caught the full force of the Chisholm charm as he added very softly, "Of one sort or another."

For a breathless moment, they stood staring at each other, then Jase broke the spell. Looking down, he gently caught one of her hands and inspected it, slowly caressing the red, chapped skin with his thumb.

His touch did strange things to both her equilibrium and her pulse rate, and Susan somehow managed to control the nearly irresistible urge to lace her fingers through his. His voice was strained when he said, "You'd better get some cream on them." He released her hand and went over to the small fridge where he kept his veterinarian supplies. He took out a white tube, and still refusing to meet her gaze he came back to the counter and squeezed a liberal amount into her palm. "It's Vitamin E cream. It should help."

There was a strange tightness in her chest as she watched him return to the fridge and replace the tube. Absently smoothing the cream into her hands, she studied his face for some clue as to what was going through his mind. His full mouth was pulled into an unyielding line, and there was an unusual tenseness about him that she found particularly distressing. He seemed so isolated, and Susan had a sudden need to comfort him. And for her that was a dangerous feeling. She knew she had a strong maternal instinct, but when she started feeling that way about a man who was as sexually attractive, as compelling as Jason Chisholm was, she was in very big trouble.

She found that her voice was treacherously unsteady when she suddenly found the courage to broach a topic that had been troubling her. "Clayton pushed the issue over me, didn't he? You didn't want me here, did you?"

There was a bleak look in Jason's eyes as he turned to face her. He stared at her for a moment, then answered in a strained tone. "No, I didn't." As if drawn against his will, he came over to her, and as though he were fighting a losing battle with himself, he trailed his knuckles along her jaw, his touch gentle. "I still don't think it's a good idea," he said, his voice low. "But for entirely different reasons, now."

CHAPTER THREE

SUSAN SPENT MOST of that night staring at the ceiling, trying to sort through some disturbing thoughts and even more disturbing feelings. But she hadn't come to grips with anything. Except that she was strongly attracted to Jason Chisholm. And that didn't solve anything, either, though it certainly did ruin any chances she might have had of falling asleep. She felt as if she'd been flattened by a ten-ton truck when her alarm finally forced her out of bed the next morning.

She managed the routine of breakfast out of sheer habit, but it wasn't until she'd had four cups of coffee and a cold shower that she felt more alive than dead. She finished tidying up the kitchen, made a batch of muffins and a stew for dinner and did the crossword in a two-week-old *Calgary Herald* before she gave in to her restlessness.

If she was going to put him and what he'd said out of her mind, she was going to have to find something physical to do, something where she could put her body in gear and her thoughts in neutral. What she needed, she thought wryly, was a load of gravel to shovel.

She finally went outside and found a beautiful sunny spring day waiting for her; the fresh mountain breeze helped to clear away her mental cobwebs. She

watched two Stellar jays at the bird feeder for a while,
then wandered toward the back of the house. She
paused when she rounded the hedge. Walter was digging up the flower beds in the backyard, and as she
stood watching him, Susan's expression became unusually solemn.

Clayton had told her the whole story, how at the age
of ten Walter had been kicked in the head by a horse,
the injury causing irreversible brain damage. Susan
wasn't too sure how to deal with his disability. A
physical handicap was one thing; she could face that
with absolute composure. But a mentally disabled
person was something else altogether. It wasn't that his
condition repulsed her, but it did bother her. She felt
an almost unreasonable compassion for anyone who,
for whatever medical or genetic reasons, had been
cheated out of a normal existence. And Walter was
certainly one of those.

But even though she had been warned, she had not
been fully prepared. The first time she saw him with
his slow, shuffling gait and listened to his laborious
efforts to speak, she had been hit with an unexpected
wave of sadness. Sometimes life was so damned un-
fair.

The main reason she was reluctant to face him on
her own was that he communicated in a kind of verbal shorthand, and she wasn't sure she'd be able to
grasp his meaning. Susan decided the wisest thing to
do was to leave, and she was just about to go back into
the house when he turned and saw her. He smiled at
her with a mixture of shyness and uncertainty, and
feeling as if she were damned no matter what she did,
Susan returned his smile. Then, with her heart in her

shoes, she walked across the lawn to where he was working.

Dudley came bounding around the corner of the house, exuberant about having some new company. He would have jumped up on Susan, but Walter caught him by the collar and gave him a firm command to sit. That was, to Susan's way of thinking, like asking an elephant to tap dance, but Dudley surprised her and plopped down on his haunches. He tipped his head and looked at her with bright eyes, silently begging to be petted. She grinned at him as she buried her hand in his thick coat and scratched him behind his ears.

Walter was watching her, and he shook his head as Dudley sagged against her legs. "He likes you," he said haltingly.

She laughed as she ruffled the dog's fur. "He should, the way I feed him." Giving the dog another pat, she turned her attention to the flower bed where Walter was working. The freshly turned earth revealed a host of new shoots that were just pushing their way through the soil. One love Susan had inherited from her grandmother was the love of gardening, and she surveyed the beds with interest. None of the plants were up far enough to really be distinguishable, and forgetting all about her former reluctance, she began questioning Walter. "What are those shoots along there?"

He stepped back into the bed and placed the garden fork by one clump. "Columbine." He moved the fork to another. "Trollius." He indicated another. "Bachelor's buttons." Slowly he worked his way back down the bed, indicating every group of shoots and marking some that weren't even up yet. By the time they'd reached the other end, Susan had a mental picture of what this flower bed would look like at the peak of the season. It would be spectacular. From the time the first daffodils bloomed in the spring until the chrysanthemums froze in the fall, there would be a colorful array of flowers in bloom.

At the far end of the garden, there was a shallow hole with a long-handled spade stuck in it, and she pointed to it. "What are you going to put there?"

Walter shrugged and slowly shook his head. "I don't know. Maybe lythrum there...something that blooms later."

Susan nodded. "That would work. Then if you do that, why don't you move this bunch of columbine over there and put a clump of daisies here?"

There was no mistaking the twinkle in his eye as he grasped the spade, pulled it free and handed it to Susan. "Sounds fine," he said with a slow grin.

Susan stared at him for a split second then grinned back as she took the shovel. "That's not fair. Don't you know you aren't supposed to let just anybody plow around in your garden?"

"Not just anybody," he said, the twinkle intensifying. "*You*, Susan."

Susan slanted an amused, if somewhat skeptical look at him. "I think you bear watching, Walter Chisholm. I have the distinct feeling I've just been had."

He chuckled and pointed to a clump of shoots. "There're the daisies."

She shot him a knowing look. "I get the message."

He was still shaking his head and smiling as he grasped the handles of the wheelbarrow and disappeared through the hedge.

The two of them spent the next hour digging and rearranging, sometimes talking, sometimes sharing long comfortable silences. Walter wheeled in several loads of compost from an old manure pile and worked it into the soil. Susan had finished moving what they had decided to move, then dug up a huge clump of irises that needed separating. She was kneeling at the end of the garden, her hands and the knees of her jeans caked with dirt, humming to herself as she broke apart the tuberous roots.

"Don't tell me. I suppose you're going to do the fencing next."

Susan froze and swore softly under her breath, feeling suddenly cornered. There was no mistaking the undercurrent of sarcasm in Jason Chisholm's voice, and sighing in resignation, she turned to face him. "Look, Jase, I like gardening. So don't make a big deal out of something that isn't."

He was standing a short distance behind her, a familiar set to his jaw, the rest of his face obscured in the shadow of his Stetson. "You're not expected to do anything around here but cook. I thought I made that perfectly clear."

She stared at him for a moment, a hint of irritation flashing in her eyes. "Don't be a bore. What am I supposed to do between meals—crochet doilies?"

She thought she saw his mouth twitch, but his face remained expressionless. "If that's what you want to do with your free time, fine."

Her irritation escalated. "For Pete's sake, do I look like the type who gets a big thrill out of sitting in a rocking chair day after day, turning out pink-and-yellow pot holders for the church bazaar?"

"I don't know. Are you?"

She suspected he was baiting her, and ignoring his question, she pushed on. "What's wrong with my helping Walter with the gardening?"

He stared at her, his eyes narrowing. "Nothing...*if* you left it at that. But seeing the way you operate, I suspect I could end up with hollyhocks planted around the barn."

Walter appeared and set the wheelbarrow down. He glanced at Jason, then gave Susan a sly wink and said solemnly, "That would look nice, wouldn't it, Susan?"

His subtle and unexpected alliance delighted Susan and she grinned up at him, her eyes sparkling. "I think it's a great idea. We could transplant the ones behind the garage, and we could put a few clumps of delphiniums along the corrals."

Walter chuckled and nodded, and Jason riveted his full attention on him, as if he weren't quite sure if Walter was serious or not. But Walter's face was as innocent as a baby's as he disappeared around the corner of the house, and Jase glanced back at Susan. He scrutinized her intently, his contemplative tone tinged with an undercurrent of amusement as he said softly, "Why do I have this uncomfortable feeling that the two of you are turning out to be bad news?"

Still grinning, Susan stood up and dusted off the dirt that was clinging to her jeans. "Maybe it's just your suspicious nature."

His amusement grew. "Like hell."

Her gaze connected with his, and Susan experienced a galvanizing flutter as she fell victim to the laughter in his eyes. She had a sudden and nearly overpowering urge to reach out and touch him, but she drew a slow, measured breath and deliberately hooked her thumbs in the pockets of her jeans. Her voice was only slightly uneven as she said, "Walter must be ready for a coffee break. How about you?"

He was watching her with an unsettling steadiness that made her knees go weak, and Susan made herself take another deep breath. He stared at her for a second longer, then the laugh lines around his eyes crinkled in a disarming smile. "I don't suppose there's a piece of cake left to go with it?"

"Leftover cake? With this gang? You have to be kidding."

He picked up the spade and stuck it in the loosened earth then grinned and shrugged. "I thought I might get lucky."

She laughed and started toward the house. "You still might. There are fresh muffins—or at least there were."

He fell into step beside her and flashed the irresistible Chisholm dimple. "Then maybe we ought to walk faster."

Susan went into the house, and Jason went to find Walter and tell him they were stopping for coffee. By the time Jason came in and washed up, she had a fresh pot of coffee brewing and the oatmeal muffins arranged in a large basket. She had just finished setting the table and was at the fridge when he finally came into the kitchen. He dropped his Stetson on the counter by the door, and raking his hand through his thick curls, came to the table.

Her eyes were dancing as she glanced up at him. "You'd better eat fast. I think I just heard Duffy and Len ride in. If they get to the table first, you'll be out of luck."

He chuckled as he pulled out a chair and sat down. "It'll take them at least twenty minutes to get here. We're trailering the horses to where we'll be working today, and they'll have to load theirs."

Susan caught the fridge door with her elbow and swung it shut, then came to the table and set down the cream, butter and two jars of jam. "Mom used to swear that we could inhale four hours of cooking in ten seconds flat, but I think this bunch has us beat by a mile."

The spark of humor in his eyes faded, and he stared at the table, a heavily retrospective look settled on his face. He leaned back, allowing Susan to set a cup of steaming coffee in front of him, an underlying weariness in his voice as he spoke. "It shouldn't have taken a doctor to see that cooking for this crew was too much for Mattie. I should have hired someone long ago."

Susan's own expression became solemn as she recognized the self-reproach in his tone. It would have been a perfect opportunity to point out to him that there was more than just the cooking that was too much for Mattie, but she refrained and steered the conversation in a different direction. "How come you call her Mattie?"

Jason didn't answer for a moment, then sighing heavily, he looked up and gave her a wry grin. "Being the only child, that was all I ever heard her called. She never bothered to make an issue of it, and I have a sneaking suspicion that both she and Dad thought it was something to encourage. She even tried to get my kids to call her Mattie.''

Susan smiled and shook her head. ''She's quite a lady.''

His voice grew solemn as he said quietly, ''Yes, she is. I don't know what I would have done without her.''

Susan realized that the situation could get very awkward if she asked any of the questions that comment opened up, so she addressed an issue she knew she was going to have to deal with sooner or later. ''I feel very badly over this deal with Clayton, Jason. I, of all people, know what he's like when he gets an idea in his head. I should have realized that me taking this job was something he'd simply bulldozed through, regardless of how you felt about it.'' Grimacing sheepishly, she gave him a warped smile. ''He can be very…tenacious…very formidable, when anyone or anything gets in his way.''

Jason studied her for a second, then leaned forward and rested his arms on the table as he absently picked at an imperfection on the mug. A warped grin appeared, and there was a touch of wry humor in his voice. ''I think you really mean ornery and bullheaded—it's a Chisholm trait, I'm afraid. Clayton and I don't often lock horns, but we sure in hell did over that.'' He hesitated, then met her gaze directly, and she experienced a weird sensation in the pit of her stomach. His voice had a peculiar huskiness to it as he continued, ''I didn't want you out here because I figured you'd expect the Double Diamond to be some sort of glitzy dude ranch, and quite frankly, I didn't think you could handle the job."

Suppressing a smile, she said quietly, "So you thought I'd be an albatross around your neck. Is that why you bit my head off when you caught me cleaning the floor?"

He gave her a twisted grin, then looked down as he continued to toy with his cup. "Yeah, something like that."

Susan leaned forward and folded her arms on the table, her expression suddenly earnest. "I came out here expecting to work, Jason, not to have an extended vacation. I know I'm here as a cook and nothing more, but I still need to be busy. I can't stand sitting around with nothing to do, and I honestly don't mind taking over some of the work that Mattie can't handle. But I don't want to face a battle with you every time I do something other than peel potatoes."

He raised his head and stared at her, a flicker of amusement lighting his eyes. "Why do I have this feeling if I give you an inch, you'll take a mile?"

She met his gaze with a hint of defiance. "I won't."

The sparkle intensified. "You will, Susan."

"I won't."

He gave a derisive snort as he shot her a disbelieving look, then pursing back a smile, he reached for a muffin. "Don't try that innocent look on me. You know damned well the minute my back's turned, you'll be up to your neck in some project or another."

"I won't do anything without checking with you first."

"Do you really expect me to believe that?"

She stared at him, a slightly tenacious set to her chin, and he raised his eyebrows in a knowing see-what-I-mean expression. Realizing that he had her cornered, and that she'd get nowhere trying to argue her way out of it, she yielded with a grin and tipped her head in unwilling agreement. "Okay, so maybe I do get a little carried away, but you don't have to be so sensitive about it."

He buttered his muffin and reached for the apricot jam, his own jaw taking on a stubborn set. "You're here to cook, not to launch a wide scale beautification program or—" he paused for emphasis "—to prove a point."

She didn't say anything as she tried to assess her best line of attack. An idea popped into her head and she finally spoke, a devious gleam in her eye. "How about if we make a deal. I'll give Mattie some extra help, and you'll give me some riding lessons."

"I'll give you lessons anyway."

"Not unless we make a fair exchange," she said stubbornly, trying to contain her satisfaction in effectively setting him up.

He looked at her, his eyes narrowing. "I think you've been around politicians too long."

"Is it a deal?"

His mouth twitched. "We'll see."

Deciding she'd better quit while she was ahead, Susan placed a muffin on her plate and reached for the butter. They fell into a comfortable silence and Susan felt strangely content, as though she had just discovered something that filled her with a vitalizing energy. And she knew, with wry humor, that this feeling of well-being wasn't from the food she was eating.

Jason interrupted her musings. "Have you ever ridden?"

She gave him a halfhearted grin. "Some."

He nearly smiled as he responded, "Define 'some.'"

"Well," she answered with a kind of perverse candor, "I can ride into a strong wind without falling off, if that tells you anything."

He tipped his head back and laughed, and Susan experienced a sudden fizzling sensation that made her catch her breath. It was the first time she'd heard him really laugh, and the transformation in him was amazing. There was a lighthearted buoyancy that stripped years off him, and Susan was mesmerized. So, she thought dazedly, beneath the sober demeanor, beneath the solemn weight of responsibility, there was another Jason Chisholm, one who was even more appealing. And the fizzle turned into an intoxicating rush.

She drew in a deep breath, and trying to ignore the excitement shooting through her, she struggled to keep her voice steady. "It isn't that funny, Jase," she said, her tone chastising as she bit back a smile.

Leaning back in his chair, he shook his head and expelled the last of his laughter on a deep sigh, his eyes still dancing as he grinned at her. "When you put it that way, maybe you do need a few lessons."

Sensing she had an advantage, she pressed him. "Then it's a deal?"

With his elbow resting on the table, he raised his cup, intently watching her over the rim. Finally he spoke. "Okay, it's a deal. But," he added emphatically, a tone of warning in his voice, "you aren't to try to do it all. Taking care of this whole house is not your responsibility. As soon as I have time, I'm going to see about lining up a housekeeper."

Susan opened her mouth to argue with him about that, then thought better of it and decided to quit while she was ahead. He was leaning back with his arms folded across his chest, his chair balanced on its back legs as he watched her through narrowed eyes.

Susan experienced an odd flustered feeling when he gave her a knowing half smile, as if he knew exactly what had been going on in her head. He studied her a moment longer, then let the chair rock forward and land with a sharp thud, his mouth twitching. "You really had to bite your tongue on that one, didn't you?" he said, his voice tinged with humor.

She lifted her chin and gave him a prim smile. "If you want to hire a housekeeper, that's your business."

"Then why," he asked softly, "do you suddenly have that determined set to your chin?"

She cast him a quick glance. "I don't," she retorted.

"Yes, you do."

"It always sticks out that way."

The Chisholm dimple appeared. "Then heaven help us," he said in a reverent tone of voice.

Voices drifted in from the open window and the screen door slammed as the other men entered the porch. Susan made an impudent face at Jason as she pushed her chair back, and he was still grinning at her when the men came into the kitchen. There was something disturbingly intimate about the look in his eyes, and a heady warmth spread through her as she stood motionless, transfixed by an indefinable spell.

The magic lasted for an electrifying moment, then Duffy and Walter sat down at the table, and Susan forced herself to sever the connection. She tried to draw a breath past the sudden tightness in her chest as she struggled to collect her composure. If she thought she was heading for big trouble before, she thought wryly, it was nothing compared to where she was right now.

Taking another deep breath to try to calm herself, she picked up the coffeepot and went back to the table. She deliberately avoided looking at Jason as she filled Walter's and Duffy's mugs, but she was so keenly aware of his nearness that she went through the motions in a kind of daze. She refilled his cup and abruptly rammed her free hand in the back pocket of her jeans when she caught herself about to let it rest on his shoulder. His silvery hair, with its perfect blending of black and white, was a disorder of soft curls. She longed to smooth it down, but she shoved her hand deeper into her pocket instead.

Len came in as she was topping Walter's cup, and he shook his head in a gesture of approval as he shoved his mug across the table for her to fill. "This grub looks like it oughta plug a few holes. It was beginning to feel like a hell of a long time till dinner." He took a bite of muffin then reached for the butter, his eyes sparkling with sheer devilry as he grinned at her. "You're one hell of a cook, Susan. Why don't you marry me and put some fat on these scrawny bones."

She laughed as she placed the jam in front of him. "You'd better think that offer through before you make it final. I may fatten you up, but have you any idea how much I'll thin down your bank account?"

He shook his head and chuckled. "Don't seem quite sportin' that an old bronc buster should have to make that kind of trade-off."

"Susan likes to negotiate, Len," Jason offered dryly.

Susan shot him a tart look, and her stomach did a crazy flip-flop when she realized how intently he was watching her. His eyes were gleaming with an amused challenge, as though he were silently daring her to debate the issue in front of everybody. She narrowed her eyes at him.

The corners of his mouth lifted and he looked away, the fabric of his plaid shirt pulling tautly across his shoulders as he leaned forward and rested his elbows on the table. Walter glanced from Jason to Susan then back to Jason, a glitter of comprehension in his eyes. He sat stroking his chin, nodding as he muttered to himself, "Real interesting."

Susan turned, riveting her full attention on him. He gave her a guileless smile and shrugged sheepishly. "These are good muffins, Susan."

Knowing exactly what was going on in his mind, she stared at him, her hand on her hip as she said warningly, "Watch it, Walter, or I'll dig up your peonies."

The others had been talking and so had missed his quiet aside, and there was a sudden lull as the three men quickly turned their attention to the conversation between Susan and Walter. Unaware of their scrutiny, Walter shook his head and chuckled. "Then you can plant them around the barn," he retorted haltingly, with an unmistakable twinkle.

Susan laughed and shook her finger at him, and Walter chuckled again. It was apparent to the others that they were sharing some private joke, so Len and Duffy picked up their conversation where they left off. Jason remained silent as he solemnly watched Susan refill Walter's cup.

As she returned the coffeepot to the element on the coffee maker, Walter pulled a dog-eared seed catalog out of his back pocket and carefully spread it on the table, an absorbed expression on his face. She came back to the table and slipped into the chair beside him, hunching over the catalog to study the colorful illustrations. "Do you have any poppies in the garden? You know, those big orange Oriental ones? A big clump of them would look fantastic behind the blue bachelor's buttons."

He nodded. "There are some."

"Where are they?"

He gave her an impish smile. "Behind the blue bachelor's buttons."

She gave him a menacing look then grinned as she punched him playfully on the shoulder. "I'm too big to have my leg pulled, Walter Chisholm."

Duffy brushed the crumbs off the front of his shirt and glanced at Walter. "Say, Walt, I was wonderin' if you'd have a look-see at that truck of mine. It's started missin' and poppin', and it's beginning to sound like it might hiccup itself to death."

The older man nodded slowly. "This afternoon."

Susan looked at Clayton's cousin. "Sounds like you get all the fun jobs."

He shrugged, his expression bashful. "I like fixing things."

"Walter's probably the best mechanic in this here country," Duffy interjected with undisguised pride.

"There ain't nothin' he can't fix. And he's a wizard with an engine."

Susan turned to the older Chisholm, her expression one of wry humor. "A wizard's just what I need. Maybe I can bribe you into saying a few incantations over my car. I've come to the conclusion that somebody's put a hex on it."

He grinned. "Apple pie should work pretty good."

Susan stared at him blankly for a moment, then her eyes began to dance when she finally caught his drift. "I think that could be arranged."

Slapping his thighs, Len pushed his chair back from the table and stood up. "Well, I guess we'd better get back to work before I put down roots." He picked up his battered cowboy hat from the floor and settled it on his head, then nodded at Susan. "That was a mighty fine snack, Susan. Appreciate it."

Susan carried the dirty mugs to the counter, then dumped the remains of the coffee down the sink. She smiled at Len as she started loading the cups in the top rack of the dishwasher. "I was just trying to put some fat on those scrawny bones of yours."

The other men had left the table and were walking out of the kitchen when Jason paused and turned to face her. "Why don't you leave this and take a walk down to the barn with me? There're a couple of horses you should be able to ride if you want, and I'll show you what tack to use."

Her stomach did a weird little hop and a skip, and she nearly shoved the rack through the back of the dishwasher in her haste to comply with his unexpected invitation. He misread her reaction as one of desperation to get out of the house, and he cocked one eyebrow, amusement in his eyes. And for the first time in a long time, Susan felt a warm blush creep up her neck.

Shaking his head, Jason slipped on his Stetson and clapped her on the shoulder as she was about to pass in front of him. "Well," he said softly, "I'd say that just about finishes all hope for any blue-and-yellow pot holders, wouldn't you?"

The weight of his hand on her shoulder did incredible things to Susan's spine, and she felt as though her whole body were turning to warm porridge. She gave herself a quick mental lecture about reacting like a silly adolescent, then forced herself to take a deep breath before she glanced up at him. Her laugh had an odd throaty timbre to it, and her voice was slightly unsteady as she retorted, "The hopes were pretty slim to begin with, Jase."

He grinned back at her, and for one electric moment their eyes held. In that instant, Susan had the overpowering sensation that some incomplete part of her had just connected with something in him, and she felt a kind of closeness, a kind of harmony she'd never experienced with anybody else. The effect was staggering.

Jason drew in a ragged breath and his gaze slid to her mouth, his touch on her shoulder almost a caress as he said unevenly, "Then maybe we'd better make a trade—the rocking chair for a saddle." His voice was even more husky as he put pressure on her shoulder, prompting her to move. "And it could be a hell of a lot more interesting."

Susan really had to fight to gather the strength and willpower to move, and as she regretfully severed the physical contact, she felt suddenly dispossessed of the warm sense of oneness that had enveloped her. Struggling to regain at least some semblance of calm, she smoothed her hands down the front of her jeans and turned toward the door.

The screen door slammed loudly behind them, and Dudley came bounding around the corner of the house, a branch the size of a small tree hanging out of his mouth. He romped along in front of them, begging for someone to play with him.

Jason bent over and took the branch, then sent it flying in a long arch in the direction of a coppice of spruce. The dog went tearing after it and Jason hooked his thumbs on his belt buckle, an air of introspection about him.

They walked on in silence for a short distance, then he glanced at Susan. "Do you mind if I ask how come you went along with Clayton's idea?"

A light breeze caught her hair, feathering it across her face, and Susan absently tucked the strand behind her ear as she lowered her head, her expression thoughtful. There was a pensive quality to her voice as she finally spoke. "I'm not sure I really know why. I've always had a fascination for the west...but there was more to it than that." She hesitated, trying to sort out her thoughts before she went on. "When he first mentioned it to me I had no intention of coming, then something changed and I found myself really caught up in the idea." Sliding her hands into the back pockets of her jeans, she frowned slightly as she kicked a small stone off the path. "Clayton's talked about it so much, it's almost as if he's given me a sense of—I don't know how to explain it—a sense of *rightness* about this country. It was almost as though I was compelled to come and see for myself.''

''And now that you have?''

Susan looked up at him, her expression serious. ''I love it,'' she said quietly.

He held her gaze for a second, then looked away, his voice suddenly gruff. ''Yeah, so do I.''

Jason followed a trail that led into the windbreak, and Susan ducked a low-hanging branch. ''I don't know how Clayton can stay away when this country means so much to him.''

Jason's manner was somewhat brusque when he responded, ''He has his reasons.''

''I know he does.''

Jason shot her a sharp look, and Susan shrugged and gave him a sheepish grin. ''Well, I don't know *exactly*, but I have my suspicions.''

He tipped his hat forward, the shadow from the brim obscuring his eyes. ''Close, but no cigar,'' he said, his voice touched with amusement.

''Thanks,'' she said dryly. They walked on in silence for a moment, then Susan spoke again. ''What did happen, Jase?''

He glanced at her. ''Have you ever asked him?''

''No.''

''Why didn't you?''

She shrugged as she idly trailed her hand through some long grass beside the trail. ''I guess I felt I'd be intruding on his privacy—that maybe he doesn't like to talk about it.''

''He doesn't.''

''Does it have anything to do with his never marrying?''

Jason caught a small branch and stripped the leaves off it. "He was married."

Susan shot him a surprised look. "When?"

"Years ago, to a Métis girl. It caused quite a storm in the district—marrying a half-breed wasn't exactly socially acceptable then—and my grandfather nearly disowned him over it. She died of tuberculosis four or five years later, and from what I can remember it was months before Clayton came out of the back country."

A hollow feeling settled in Susan's stomach. "Do you remember her?"

"Yeah, I sure do. White Dove was the most gentle, tranquil person I've ever known. When she died, Clayton told Mattie that there would never be another woman to take her place."

Susan blinked back the sudden sting of tears. "How sad."

Jason looked at her, his eyes solemn. "No, it isn't, Susan," he said quietly. "He's had something that very few people ever find, and for the most part, he's grateful he had the time he did with her. Occasionally he gets down about it, but not very damned often."

"Memories are a poor substitute," she countered softly.

"Maybe, but I think Clayton would tell you that the memories he has are a lot better than the day-to-day existence most people live."

Susan frowned thoughtfully as she considered Jason's comment. Knowing Clayton the way she did, she knew his nephew was right. But one thing was clear: the Chisholm family had suffered its share of tragedy.

They passed through the wide belt of trees, and the rest of the ranch buildings came into view. The arena was at the most eastward end of the complex, with a series of corrals between it and a huge red barn, and on a knoll off to the west, a modern wind generator had been erected, its blades spinning soundlessly in the light breeze. Jason glanced at her, a tormenting glint in his eyes. "Too bad Clayton hadn't sent you out last year. All the buildings had to be painted, and it got to the point where I practically had to use a cattle prod on everybody to get it done. You would've had a great time."

She gave him a warning glance. "You're pushing your luck, Jason Chisholm," she said softly.

He just grinned and tipped his hat a little lower. As they walked past one of the larger outbuildings, Susan spotted several horses grazing in the field, and she slowed her pace. She had gone through a phase in her teens when she nearly drove her parents crazy begging for a horse, but she could never quite convince them that she would simply die if she didn't get one. Her delirium of enthusiasm had finally passed, but the fascination had remained, and she watched them now with genuine interest.

There was a soft whinny and she turned. A sorrel gelding was in the corral right beside the barn and he came over to the fence, his head held high and his ears pricked in interest. She started toward him, but he threw his head and shied away, then trotted off to the back corner.

She hooked her elbows on the top rail, her chin resting on her forearms as she watched him prance around. Jason leaned against the fence. "That's old

Riley. Mattie broke him over twenty years ago and he's still going strong."

Susan's expression was one of amazement. "You don't still ride him, do you?"

Jason rested his foot on the bottom rail as he braced his shoulder against the post. "Sometimes. We use him at roundup, and every once in a while Clayton saddles him up, but he's usually turned loose in the big pasture. The only reason he's in here now is because he needs his hooves trimmed."

He gave a low whistle and the horse threw his head, then trotted over to the rail and nuzzled Jason's shoulder. Jason smiled and rubbed the animal's nose. "Mattie and he used to have some rare old go-arounds. He shies at anything that moves, and he used to pile her regularly. I think it eventually developed into a simple battle of wills."

Susan slowly stroked the gelding's neck as she listened to Jason, her eyes sparkling. When he finished, she shook her head and laughed, a look of pure mischief on her face. "It sounds as if the Chisholm contrariness is a common characteristic around here, doesn't it?"

Jason turned his head and looked at her, a warning tone in his voice. "Don't push *your* luck, lady, or you'll be back in the kitchen."

She shook her head, her hands raised in a gesture of refusal. "Not a chance."

With a hint of a smile, he straightened and motioned toward the barn. "Come on. I'll show you around."

Inside, a fragrance of horses and dried hay rose up to meet her, and Susan squinted, waiting for her eyes to adjust to the dim interior. There was a tack room inside the door, and with one quick glance at the large box stalls lining the structure, Susan followed Jason into the small room. A number of specially built brackets mounted on the wall held all the saddles, each with a saddle blanket draped over it. On the end wall two rows of wooden knobs held a variety of halters, bridles and martingales, and along the bottom of a row of shelves stood several pairs of boots.

Dust motes hung suspended on the shaft of light that slanted in through the grimy window, and a large white cat lay in the splash of brightness that fell across an old sheepskin saddle pad.

Jason flipped a halter off a hook, then indicated the boots. "You should be able to find a pair that'll fit you. And do wear them, Susan," he cautioned. "Wearing shoes without heels is asking for trouble."

She nodded, and he turned away. Draping the halter over his shoulder, Jason stuck his hand into a large bag then handed her the huge pellets he'd picked up. "I'll give you Breezy to ride, and she'll come in with a whistle if you use the right bait."

Susan followed him out of the tack room, and as Jason headed for the other end of the barn, she fell into step with him. "How many horses do you have?"

"I have about fifty head right now, but ten of those have been sold to an oilman from the States. He wants to try them out as polo ponies. They'll be shipped out in another couple of weeks, as soon as they've shed out." He slid open the big door at the end of the barn and they stepped out into the sunlight. "Can you whistle?"

She nodded and gave him a dubious look.

He let out two shrill whistles and the horses in the field raised their heads, but one started loping toward the barn. Jason turned and smiled, an almost sheepish look on his face. "Well, it beats walking out there to get them."

Susan suppressed a smile. "Sure it does." She extended her hand as the horse trotted up, and Breezy eagerly nuzzled the pellets out of her palm.

Speaking quietly, Jason slipped the halter, which was made of a sturdy red twill, over the horse's head. "Do you want to take her for a ride now?"

She glanced at her watch and shook her head. "I won't have time. I still have to make lunch for you to take with you."

Patting the mare on the shoulder, Jason unsnapped the shank from the halter, then turned the horse loose. "I'll leave the halter on so it'll be easier to catch her."

Susan watched the horse gallop off, her eyes glowing with pleasure. She turned to say something to Jason, and her heart flip-flopped when she found him watching her with solemn eyes, an unfathomable expression on his face. The wind feathered her hair across her cheek and as if drawn against his will, Jason reached out to smooth it back. Before he actually touched her, he hauled in a deep breath and turned away, his voice uneven. "I'd better get going. Len and Duff will be waiting for me."

And an aching emptiness overcame Susan as she watched him walk away.

CHAPTER FOUR

THE REST OF THE AFTERNOON passed in a daze. Susan was actually relieved when the kids finally got home from school, bringing with them enough commotion to distract anybody. She'd spent most of the day trying not to think about their father, which was a lost cause. She tried to rationalize her way out of it, block it out, then finally tried to sweat it out by scrubbing down both bathrooms in the main house. But that didn't work, either. At least at the rate things were going, two more encounters with Jase Chisholm and she'd have the whole house cleaned from top to bottom.

The only thing that snapped her back to reality was when Michael came racing in the back door, wound up like a top because Todd had a snake—a green snake with dots on its back that wriggled when you squeezed it. And Todd, being a normal, red-blooded boy, was threatening to stuff it down his brother's neck. By the time Susan caught Todd as he tore by, hauled him up short and discovered the snake was a rubber one, she had so much adrenaline racing through her system that *nothing* affected her.

She confiscated the snake, made the boys set the table and listened to Lucy try to list all the words that rhymed with "stink." It wasn't until she had the potatoes peeled and on the stove that it dawned on her she hadn't seen Patricia. Drying her hands on her jeans, she went into the main house and finally found the girl huddled in a big chair in the living room, sobbing her heart out.

A look of concern crossed Susan's face as she crouched beside her and smoothed back her hair. "What's the matter, Trish? Did something happen on the way home from school?"

Patricia vehemently shook her head, sobs racking her whole body, and Susan made a sympathetic sound as she slipped her arms around the teenager and cuddled her to her. "Come on, honey. Stop crying and tell me what's wrong. Maybe I can help."

The girl buried her head against Susan's shoulder, her flood of tears soaking through her blouse. Susan's expression was very solemn as she gently rocked her, remembering how much things hurt at that age. She pressed her face into the child's hair, her tone gentle as she murmured, "Did somebody say something or did something happen?"

Patricia dragged in a ragged breath, her voice muffled and distorted by weeping as she ground out vehemently, "I hate being fat! I hate it! I'm tired of everybody poking fun at me, and I'm tired of pretending it doesn't matter." She burst into a fresh flood of tears. "Because it does matter. It does!"

Susan cuddled her closer and kissed her on the forehead. "I know it matters, Trish. I was really overweight when I was your age, and I hated it, too. And everybody thinks because you're fat, you're supposed to be a good sport about it."

Wiping her face with the back of her hand, Patricia pulled out of Susan's embrace, her weeping suddenly checked. She wiped her nose on a balled-up tissue then raised her head. Her face was splotchy and swollen and her mouth was puffy, and she looked utterly miserable. But there was the tiniest glimmer of hope in her eyes as she looked at Susan. "Were you really, Susan? Fat, I mean? You're so tall and slim now."

Susan suppressed a smile as she brushed back wispy strands of hair that were clinging to the girl's face. "Yes, I was, Trish. And I hated it, too."

Patricia wiped her nose again then looked down as she agitatedly twisted the Kleenex into a rope. "One of the neighbors up the road—I baby-sit for them all the time—she joined Weight Watchers last year and she said I could go with her. But Grandma didn't want me to go. She said wanting to be thin was silly and that it was a waste of money and that I'd slim down in my own good time. I said I would pay for it with my baby-sitting money, but she said no."

"Did you talk to your dad about it?"

Patricia lifted her head and met Susan's gaze. "I tried, and I think he would have let me go if it hadn't been for Grandma. But he didn't want to upset her."

Susan frowned and chewed absently on her bottom lip. "I see," she said thoughtfully.

"Mrs. Donaldson gave me the books so I could go on the diet by myself, but every time Grandma caught me measuring my servings, she'd get all worried. She was afraid I was going to turn anorexic or something." Sighing tremulously, Patricia lowered her head. "I really love Grandma, and I didn't want to do anything that was going to upset her so I quit trying."

There was a look of speculation on Susan's face as she stared at the child. "Do you still have the books?"

"Yes."

"Will you get them for me?"

Patricia stared at the woman's face. "Why?"

"Well, I don't want to do anything to upset your grandmother either, Patricia, but I think we can work this without anyone ever knowing. We won't be able to say anything to anybody, and we'll have to be careful, but I think we can do it."

For a moment, Patricia continued to stare at her, then her eyes filled with tears again, only this time they were tears of happiness, and she flung her arms around Susan's neck and hugged her fiercely. "Oh, Susan, I'll do anything—*anything*—if you'll just help me."

There was an odd tightness in Susan's throat, and she tried to overcome it before she answered, "Well, the first thing you can do is go get the books."

Patricia gave her another hug, then scrambled off the chair and went flying up the stairs, her eyes bright. Susan sighed and slapped her thighs as she stood up. "Wonderful," she muttered to herself. "Now I'm conspiring with a child behind her grandmother's back." She felt a sharp twinge of conscience as she walked out of the living room, but she was still going to help the kid, conscience or not.

By the time supper was ready, Susan had read the pamphlets, fixed a scribbler for a daily record book, noted Patricia's weight and had a week's worth of school lunches planned. And Patricia was floating on air.

Todd looked at his sister, who was happily humming to herself as she made the salad for supper, his expression suspicious. "What's the matter with her? Why's she so happy, anyway?"

Susan patted him on the head and answered him airily, "Why, Toddy! She's all happy because she gets to go to your baseball game tonight."

He rolled his eyes heavenward and muttered, "Gimme a break."

"Would that be one leg or two?"

Todd screwed up his face in total incomprehension. Then the lights went on in his eyes and he let out a hoot of laughter. "Gimme a break—one leg or two! One leg or two!" He flopped on a chair and tipped his head back, convulsing with a fit of giggles. "I'm gonna remember that. I am."

Susan watched him with a wry smile, or at least she did until it hit her how much he looked like his father, then she gave herself a stern mental shake and went to mash the potatoes. She was whipping them with a mixer when Mattie came, the traces of sleep still on her face. She shook her head in disbelief, her tone apologetic. "I don't know what's come over me, Susan. I truly don't. I've done nothing but sleep since you've arrived."

Susan smiled at her as she switched off the appliance. "There's no need to apologize, Mattie. I'm having a great time bossing everyone around."

The older woman attempted a facsimile of a stern expression as she surveyed her grandchildren. "Well, they certainly could do with a little bossing."

Michael grinned at her as he carried the buns to the table. "You're so mean, Grandma." He set the basket down then looked back at his grandmother. "Are you going to come to our baseball game tonight? We're playing High River and I'm going to pitch."

Weariness flashed across the older woman's face, and Susan was about to intercede, but Todd beat her to it. "It's okay if you don't come, Grandma. Honest. Susan and Uncle Walter are coming, and Dad said he would really try to make it later."

Mattie sat down at the table, a conscience-stricken look on her face. Michael went over and put his arms around her shoulders and gave her a little hug. "Maybe it'd be better if you didn't come, then I won't feel so dumb if I mess up."

Mattie smiled at him and gave his hand an affectionate pat. "You'll do just fine, Michael. But maybe I will stay home if you really don't mind. I'm so very tired."

He smiled reassuringly. "It's okay, really. Maybe Todd and I will mess up so bad, we'll spend the whole game sitting on the bench."

Mattie shook her head in amused affection as she sighed wearily. "That would be worth watching, Mikey. I don't think I've ever seen you just *sit*."

THE CHISHOLM FAMILY VEHICLE was a big nine-passenger Suburban, and Susan felt as if she were behind the wheel of a tank after her Volkswagen Beetle. She had not expected to drive, but Walter had handed her the keys and shook his head when she tried to hand them back.

He gave her directions, and by the time they arrived at the ball diamond, several other vehicles were already parked along the road. Susan felt a little hesitant as they approached a group of parents who had gathered behind the team bench.

But Michael would have no part of that. He caught her hand and dragged her into the group, a big grin on his face. "Hey, guys, this is Pete Lynton's sister and she works for my Uncle Clayton."

Several people turned to look, and Susan felt as if he'd just put her on sale. An extremely attractive woman in her mid-thirties approached her, smiling at Susan as if they were old friends. "Well, hi there. You must be Susan. I'm Carol Redding. We live just up the road from the Double Diamond."

Susan took her outstretched hand and smiled back. The three Redding boys spent considerable time with the Chisholms, and they had the same open smile as their mother. Carol introduced her to everyone, and in less than ten minutes she felt as comfortable as she would at a community gathering at home.

There was a swarm of boys milling around in blue-and-gray striped uniforms with Dodgers' crests on them, and the coach, a big man with a booming voice, clapped Susan on the shoulder. "I'm short some help tonight. How would you feel about warming this crew up, Pete Lynton's sister? And if you're as good as Todd says you are, we'll hire you," he added with a hearty laugh.

She laughed, and still feeling somewhat conspicuous, pulled a bat out of the equipment bag and picked up three balls, then went to stand at home plate. Signaling for the stocky redheaded catcher to catch for her, she started batting infield flies. If anyone had any doubts about her qualifications, they were soon dispelled as she expertly peppered the field with a mixture of grounders and line drives.

"Hey Wilson," somebody yelled at the coach. "Give us a break and play your new assistant."

Susan glanced over to the first-base base line. A tall blond man was watching her, his arms folded across his chest, an unholy grin splitting his face. He was one of those lean wiry men who had a certain athletic grace about them—tough and with endless stamina, and who stood out in a crowd. Only this one *really* stood out with his Robert Redford good looks and an utterly engaging grin.

She was so busy watching him, she missed an incoming ball, and he shook his head, his expression schooled into one of woe. "Geez, I don't know about these imports, Wilson."

The agonized look on his face made her laugh, and Susan missed another incoming ball. The catcher rolled his eyes heavenward and muttered something about dopey women.

By then, the opposing team had arrived, and with a signal from Mr. Wilson, the Dodgers trotted in from the field. Susan caught a ball with one already in her hand, then tossing the bat to Todd started walking toward the bench.

The blonde was watching her, a truly wicked sparkle in his eyes. When she got close enough, he stuck out his hand and introduced himself. "I'm Tyler Redding. All those Redding boys who hang around the Double Diamond are my nephews."

Susan had already suspected he was the much talked about Tyler Redding, and she had certainly heard enough about him. He was a championship chuckwagon driver and had, for two years in a row, taken top money at the Calgary Stampede, his fame making him an idol for both his nephews and the Chisholm boys.

She smiled and took his hand. "I'm Susan Lynton."

He nodded, his lips pursed. "So I've heard." He grinned at her suddenly, flashing a set of perfect teeth. "You're some ball player."

She grinned back. "You're some heckler."

He watched her intently, his grin turning into a thoughtful half smile. "So," he said softly, as though he were thinking out loud, "this is the reason ol' Jase is in a sweat."

Feeling as though he had suddenly poured ice water over her, she stared at him, her expression frozen. She felt at an utter loss for words, and she turned away, trying to cover up her discomfort. Needing something to do, she knelt by the equipment bag and started arranging bats on the ground.

Tyler squatted beside her, his voice suddenly quiet and serious. "I apologize for that crack. Sometimes I put my mouth in gear while my brain's still in neutral."

Before she thought about what she was saying, she answered sharply, "Yes, you do."

That made him laugh and she glanced up at him as he shook his head, his voice still heavy with laughter. "Man, you're a flinty one, aren't you?"

"I try," she answered wryly.

He laughed again. Then his expression grew serious as he studied her and added thoughtfully, "I think something worthwhile has finally turned up in Jase Chisholm's life.''

There was nothing flip about his observation, and it took Susan a second before it registered that he meant every word. She didn't know quite how to respond or what to say, and she fingered one of the bats before she looked up at him. "I think I'll take that as a compliment," she said, trying to smile.

He nodded. "You do that," he said quietly. "It was sure in hell meant as one." He continued to watch her for a moment, then clapped her lightly on the shoulder and stood up. "See you around, Susan Lynton." And she watched him walk away, a funny sensation settling inside her.

It was the top of the third inning when Susan's internal antennae started tingling, and she glanced around. Jason had just arrived and was standing with Tyler and Walter behind the team bench. Lucy distracted her as she came running up behind her and looped her arms around her neck, then leaned against Susan's back. Right then, the boy who was batting for the Dodgers hit a pop fly to center field, making the third out for the inning. Lucy continued to hang off Susan's neck, bobbing her head in time to the music as she made up words to a song she was singing under her breath.

The Dodgers took the field, and Susan's expression changed as she watched Michael pitch. Unfortunately the first two batters got on base because of outfield errors, but even so, Michael was doing a very credible job. The third batter came up, and Susan could tell by the way he settled himself at the plate that this kid was fully capable of bringing those two runs home. Michael's expression became more intense, then with his face twisted in concentration he made his pitch. One strike. He wound up again, and as soon as he let the ball go, Susan knew it was a hit.

The batter connected with sizzling line drive to the left of the shortstop, but somehow Todd, who was well behind the baseline, managed to stretch out and trap it in his glove, the velocity of the ball yanking him off his feet and rolling him over. He came up with the ball still clutched in his glove, a dazed look on his face as the runner who was headed for third whirled to return to second. Susan yelled for a triple play, and Todd reacted, firing the ball to second base. The second baseman made the tag and fired the ball to first, catching the other runner.

But there was no elation on Susan's face as she disconnected Lucy's arms and got to her feet. She knew by the way Todd had caught the ball and by the look on his face that he had really hurt his hand. He was fighting to hold back tears as he came to the bench, his face white.

Susan knelt down in front of him as she carefully slipped off his glove. "Did you catch it on the ends of the fingers or did they get bent back?"

"Bent back," he whispered as he inhaled sharply.

Susan winced when she saw that the fingers were already starting to turn purplish. "I wish we had some ice. If we could stop that swelling, we could tape them so you could finish the game."

Jason crouched beside her and inspected his son's hand. "Bring him over to Redding's car. Carol has a cooler of pop for the kids in the trunk, and she said there was plenty of ice in it."

Susan glanced at Todd. "Okay, Todd? How about we do that?"

He nodded, his face even more ashen than before. She picked up his glove and stood up, then put her arm around his shoulders, gently guiding him toward the parked cars. By the time they reached the vehicle, Jason had the cooler lifted out and the lid open.

Taking Todd's arm by the wrist, she carefully submerged his hand in the chipped ice and gently packed it around his fingers. The boy looked up at her, his eyes dark against his waxen face. "I won't be able to finish the game, will I? I'm one of the best batters on our team, and we're ahead by one, and I won't be able to play. Maybe we could beat them this time."

Crouching beside his son, Jason draped an arm around the boy's hips. "You've sprained your fingers pretty bad, son. Your hand's going to be really sore, and if they swell much more, you aren't going to be able to hold the bat."

With an age-old maternal gesture, Susan lightly brushed his damp hair off his forehead and then let her hand rest on his shoulder. "That was a great play you made, Todd," she said as she gave him a reassuring shake. "If you hadn't hung on to that ball, they'd have scored two runs—and just think, you put three out in one play."

Todd shrugged with embarrassment then grinned at her. "I heard you yell 'go for the triple' and I figured I'd better make it or else."

She ruffled his hair and stood up. "Or else is right." She lifted his hand and looked at it, then she grinned down at him. "Well, at least you didn't sprain all four fingers. By the looks of it, there are only two that are really bad."

He looked up at her, his expression hopeful. "I can still play, Susan. Honest I can. They don't hurt that bad."

There was a doubtful look in her eyes as she smoothed her hand down his arm. Uncertain about what to say, she glanced at Jason and found him watching her, his head tipped to one side, a strange contemplative expression on his face. His eyes remained unreadable for a moment, then he smiled and said, "Seeing you're the expert on sprained fingers, what do you think?"

She grimaced then crouched and rechecked Todd's hand. "Well, if we can get our hands on some of the stretchy adhesive tape, I can strap his fingers so he'll be able to play." She looked at Todd, her tone warning as she said, "I can tape them so they won't get sprained any worse, but it's going to really hurt if they get hit again."

He thought about it for a minute then grinned. "I can stand it."

His father smiled and stood up. "Okay, kid. Then let's go."

Jason put the cooler back in the trunk, and they walked toward the bench. There was a large first-aid kit by the equipment bag, and Susan sank to her knees and opened it.

Todd crouched beside her, a conspiratorial tone in his voice as he whispered, "I thought I'd dropped the ball when I fell. It wasn't until you yelled I realized I still had it in my glove. Boy, was I surprised."

Jason overheard him, and handing Susan the roll of tape, he gave his son an amused glance. "You weren't the only one."

Tipping his head back, the boy squinted up at his dad, a pleased look on his face. "It *was* a pretty good catch, wasn't it, Dad? Just like a real shortstop."

Susan bit back a smile. "Then why were you standing there if you weren't the real shortstop?"

He gave her a playful punch on the shoulder. "You know what I mean."

Jason glanced down at her and shook his head, a glint of laughter in his eyes. "Maybe he ought to stick to saving baseball cards."

Michael came tearing over and dropped down by his father, his face flushed and slightly grimy as he crowded in next to Todd. "Are you still gonna be able to play? You gotta play." Then his face lit up with an enraptured grin. "That was some catch! And a real triple play! Wow! Just like a real shortstop."

Susan's gaze connected with Jason's, and somehow she managed not to laugh as he raised his eyes to the heavens in a beseeching gesture, then cleared his throat and turned away. "I'll go tell the coach you're still in the game."

Susan forced her face into a deadpan expression as she deliberately lowered her head over Todd's hand.

Michael crowded closer to scrutinize his brother's hand. "That's gonna hurt, isn't it?"

"Nah," Todd said nonchalantly, trying to seem totally disinterested.

There was a flash of amusement in Susan's eyes. One thing she'd learned over the years was that small boys would rather die than admit to pain. Very carefully, she shaped his swollen fingers into a slight curve, and Todd sucked in his breath sharply. She glanced up at him and gave him a reassuring look. "If I tape them with the right curve on them, you'll be able to hang on to the bat and still be able to get your glove on." She dried off his hand on the tail of her blouse, adjusted the position of his fingers and started wrapping. "I'm going to tape all your fingers together. That way, the two good ones will act as a splint, so if you do get hit again, you won't sprain them any more."

Todd let his breath go as he watched with interest. "Did you used to tape your brother's hands when he got a sprain?"

She could tell by the tingle down her spine that Jason was back and was standing very close to her. His presence unnerved her, and she fumbled clumsily with the strip of tape, accidentally twisting it so that it adhered to itself. Crouching beside her, he reached over and straightened the tape, his hands making contact with hers. A frantic fluttering in her chest paralyzed her lungs, and she had to fight to draw a breath.

"Well, did you?"

It took a second for her to collect her wits enough to answer him. "Not often. It was usually me who got all the sprains. He just stood out there firing fast balls at me."

"Wow," Todd said in awed tones. "Just think, you used to catch for Pete Lynton."

Susan cast him a slightly caustic look. "I used to do his dirty laundry, too, but I don't suppose you view that with quite the same reverence."

Jason grinned as he held the tape where Susan indicated. "Hardly. As far as Todd's concerned, clean clothes are something that just miraculously happen. It doesn't have the same glamour at all."

Todd grimaced. "Aw, come on, Dad. I'm not that bad."

"Nearly." Jason turned over his son's hand and smoothed down the tape. "You must've sprained a lot of fingers to develop this technique."

"I did. My mother was convinced I was a confirmed tomboy and that my femininity would never amount to a hill of beans."

His voice had a sudden husky texture to it and he said softly, "Didn't your mother ever tell you there's something very appealing about a tomboy?"

She was transfixed by his amused gaze, and Susan felt as if everything were going into a long slow spin, leaving her light-headed. "My mother was too busy wallowing in despair over my lack of social graces."

Todd broke the spell. "Michael's up to bat. Can I go watch?"

Tearing her eyes away and collecting her wits, Susan cut free the roll of tape, her voice unusually low. "Sure. But Todd, I want you to watch the pitcher. He has a favorite slot for right-handed batters. About every third pitch, he throws one that just catches the corner of the plate low and inside. If you widen your stance and wait for that one pitch, you should be able to put it over the fence. And with that angle of swing, you won't put too much strain on your hand."

He grinned at her and scrambled to his feet. "Right, Coach!"

Brushing the dried grass off her slacks, she stood up and watched him go, keenly aware of his father standing beside her. She expected Jason to rejoin

Walter and Tyler, but he remained beside her, his hands rammed in the back pockets of his jeans, his legs locked, his attention focused on his younger son. She studied his profile for a second, then turned her attention to Michael.

Michael got on base with a clean grounder to third and flashed Susan and Jason a delighted smile from first, then bent over, his hands on his knees, trying his best to look like a "real" ball player.

When Todd came up to bat, there were two out and two on base, and Susan's expression became intent. Jason grinned down at her. "You'll hear about this for the rest of your natural life if you're wrong, you know."

She grimaced. "I know."

The first pitch was a perfect strike across the middle of the plate, but Todd let it go by, then glanced at Susan, his expression questioning. She reassured him with a nod and he turned back to face the pitcher. The second pitch was a ball, and the third, true to Susan's scouting, was low and inside, and Todd connected. As soon as he made contact, he winced and yanked his hand away, an expression of pain flitting across his face as he headed for first. The ball sailed away over the left field fence as she had predicted.

Jason raised his eyebrows in surprise, then looked at Susan. "Have you ever considered the fact that maybe you're in the wrong business?"

She laughed and shrugged. "I'm always in the wrong business." Just then Walter came over to Jason, a strange glazed look in his eyes. Jason spoke to him quietly, then handed him the keys to his truck, his expression one of concern as he watched the older man walk away.

Susan looked up at him. "Is something wrong?"

He sighed and shook his head. "Not really. He just wants to go home. He has spells occasionally when he develops very severe headaches, and when that happens he just wants to go off by himself."

Susan was going to question him further about Walter's condition, but she changed her mind when she saw the taut look around Jase's mouth. She suspected that there weren't many days when Jason wasn't reminded, in one way or another, of the enormous family responsibilities he shouldered.

By the time they returned to the Double Diamond, it was very late. Lucy had fallen asleep on Susan's lap during the long drive home, and even the boys had finally wound down from their much sought-after win.

As they pulled into the driveway, Susan gently shifted Lucy's weight as she slipped the girl's arms around her shoulders, then glanced at Jason. "If you want to check on Walter, I'll get the kids to bed."

He parked beside the caragana hedge and switched off the lights and ignition before he answered her. "I think I'd better. He sometimes forgets his medicine when he's like that." He opened the door and turned to get out. "I'll carry Lucy in first."

"No, that's okay. I can manage. You go ahead."

He stared at her for a moment, the interior light in the vehicle casting his face in dark shadows, then he nodded and climbed out, closing the door behind him.

Subdued by sleepiness, the two boys trailed into the house behind Susan as Patricia held the door open for her. With Lucy draped over her shoulder and still dead to the world, Susan entered the darkened porch, then addressed Patricia in a whisper. "There's a bunch of carrot and celery sticks in a plastic bag in the fridge, and there's some salad left from supper in a little white container. You can have those if you want, Trish, and you can have one more glass of milk."

Patricia opened the door leading into the main house and turned on the kitchen light. "Thanks, Susan," she whispered gratefully. "I was getting so hungry."

"You go have your snack, then you better come right up to bed, okay?"

"Okay."

Lucy stirred and twisted her head on Susan's shoulder, and the woman cuddled her closer as she turned toward the living room and the stairs. "Shh, honey. We'll have you in bed in just a minute."

The boys were dragging themselves toward their room as Susan came upstairs. "You guys make sure you brush your teeth before you go to bed, okay?"

"Aw, Susan."

"Teeth first," she whispered firmly as she turned down the hallway toward Lucy's room. She heard them grumbling as they entered the bathroom.

Patricia had already come upstairs by the time Susan had Lucy ready for bed, and she heard the older girl speak to someone before her bedroom door closed. Susan listened for a minute then bent over the sleeping child and gently brushed back the dark tumble of curls. She tucked the comforter around her and shut off the small night-light.

When Susan turned around, Jason was standing in the doorway, his hand resting on the knob, his body silhouetted against the light from the hallway. Silently she slipped out of the darkened room, inadvertently brushing against him as she passed in front of him. The physical contact set off a flurry of electric sensations within her, and she felt him tense. Without looking at him, Susan went quietly downstairs, trying not to let her suddenly wanton thoughts get the best of her.

Jason followed her down and paused by the living-room bookshelves, a pronounced set to his jaw. Sensing he had something to say, Susan hesitated, a strange anticipation unfolding in her.

There was a certain edginess about him, as though he were dealing with a very awkward situation, and his hands weren't quite steady as he rolled back the cuffs of his shirt. "I want to thank you for going out of your way for the boys tonight," he said quietly, an odd huskiness to his voice. There was a strained hesitation, then he finally raised his gaze and looked at her, his eyes dark and very solemn. "It meant a lot to them having you there. I think they sometimes feel a little left out because they're the only kids on the team who don't have a mother there rooting for them."

His frankness touched a disturbingly responsive cord in her, and suddenly needing something to keep her hands occupied, Susan picked up Lucy's sweater from the arm of the sofa and began folding it. "It wasn't any big sacrifice on my part," she responded, her own voice uneven. "It was a good game and I really enjoyed it." She finally raised her eyes to meet his, the intensity radiating between them sapping her of strength. She could feel her pulse accelerate as she took a slow breath, then murmured, "You've got a good bunch of kids, Jase. You can really be proud of them.''

He looked down and refolded one sleeve, his voice so strained she could barely hear him. ''I am.''

There was something in his voice that made her long to go to him, as if some force were drawing them together.

Nor was she the only one affected. She sensed he was fighting to hold his distance, but knowing that only intensified her overwhelming feelings. It was as though they were separated by some chasm that was impossible to span.

It seemed that they stood there forever, neither of them speaking, the silence compounding the tension between them. Unable to endure it any longer, Susan finally screwed up her courage. ''I think we need to talk, Jason,'' she whispered.

He had moved away and stood staring out the window, his arm braced against the frame, an unyielding set to his profile. There was a strained silence, then he answered raggedly, ''I think it's better if we don't.''

It didn't take much insight to realize he was experiencing feelings he was having trouble dealing with, and Susan gazed at him, a nearly suffocating ache unfolding inside her. She wanted so badly to go to him, but she also knew she didn't dare. She realized it was going to be up to her to lighten the tension between them, so she said softly, ''If we can't talk, how about a coffee and a piece of pie?''

He made no response for several moments, then finally he turned and looked at her, a halfhearted grin creasing his face. ''How about a riding lesson instead?''

Her eyes lit up. "Are you serious? It's not too late?"

There was a touch of wry humor in his eyes as he said gruffly, "It might be too late if we stay in this house."

For some reason, his reply uncorked an incredible effervescence inside her, and she laughed, a heady sensation bubbling through her. "I think you're a coward, Jason Chisholm."

The tense look left his face and he grinned back at her. "Under the circumstances, I'd rather think of myself as prudent." They were standing close enough for the fragrance of him to fill her senses, but what she was feeling toward him went far beyond simple physical attraction. It was much deeper than that, and she was finally forced to face the real reason that she had this unholy need to be close to him, to touch him. Susan knew right then and there that she was utterly lost. She had already fallen in love with him; it was that plain and simple.

CHAPTER FIVE

"CAN I, SUSAN? Can I? Grandma said I could if it was all right with you."

Susan gave her head a shake and stared vacantly down at Lucy, who was hopping around, anxiously waiting for the verdict. Not having heard one word the child had said, she exhaled sharply as she leaned against the sink and focused on the little girl. "Can you what?"

Lucy gave a sigh of exasperation and repeated her question. "Can I bring the box of old curtains down from the attic? I want to play dress-up with them, and Grandma said I could if it was all right with you."

"I don't see why not, as long as you promise to clean up your room first."

Lucy skipped off, her curls bobbing in agreement. "I promise."

Susan turned back to the counter and stared down bewilderedly at the bowl of ingredients sitting there. For the life of her, she could not remember what she'd already added to the batter, and she knew if she didn't get it finished soon, she wouldn't even be able to guarantee what it was supposed to be.

With an absent look in her eyes, she started mixing in two eggs, her thoughts drifting back to the night before. The few hours she'd spent with Jason had been, quite simply, the best few hours she'd ever spent in her life. Once he relaxed his guard a little, she'd found out what the real Jason Chisholm was all about. Not only did he possess a keen sense of humor and an inquiring mind, but she discovered he had a down-to-earth philosophy that she fully appreciated.

But there had been more than that. When they'd left the arena after the lesson, Susan had been over-whelmed by the brilliant canopy of stars that hung overhead, and she'd gazed up, transfixed by the wonder of it. Unwilling to go in on such a perfect night, she had poked along, fascinated by the heavens and how close they'd seemed. Jason had started pointing out various constellations and somehow or another, they ended up watching the heavenly display from a stack of bales, the fragrance of hay and the silence of darkness enveloping them. In the privacy of night, each had the chance to quietly discover the fiber of the other, and in that short space of time, Susan felt closer to him than she'd ever felt to another human being. And not in one of her past relationships had she ex-perienced the kind of easy compatibility she'd felt with him.

It hadn't been until she climbed into bed that her euphoria betrayed her, allowing intimate and provoc-ative fantasies to infiltrate her mind. She lay there in the dark, acutely aware that he was lying just on the other side of the wall, less than an arm's length away. But it wasn't the physical act of loving him that she longed for; rather the simple, almost unbearable need to have him hold her.

"How come the batter's all lumped over on one side? Is it supposed to be like that?"

Susan snapped out of her reverie with a jerk and stared down at Michael, who was standing by the counter, his head propped in his hand, watching what she was doing with considerable interest. "What's it going to be?"

Susan smiled lopsidedly as she had a good look at the concoction in the bowl. "Who knows?" she answered dryly.

"Can I lick the beaters when you're done?"

"Have you finished cleaning up your room?"

He pulled a rueful face. "Are you gonna make us clean our rooms *every* Saturday?"

"Do you want me to help you with your pitching?"

He gave her a grin that was intended to melt her heart. "I could do it one Saturday and Todd could do it the next," he offered hopefully.

She stared down at him. "Wrong. You can clean up your own messes, Michael Matthew, and quit hauling out the Chisholm charm." She removed the beaters from the mixer and held them in her hand. "Now, is your room done?"

"Yes."

"Vacuumed and dusted?"

He licked his lips in anticipation. "Yes."

"The bed's made and your laundry's gathered up?"

"Yes."

"Okay, then. Here you go. One for you and one for your brother."

"What about Lucy and Patricia?"

"Lucy gets the bowl when she'd done her chores, and Patricia doesn't want any."

"Can I have her share?"

Susan glanced down at him, biting back a smile as she poured the batter into a cake tin. "What a little pig."

Michael grinned and shrugged. "Dontcha know I'm a growing boy?"

"Yes, Grandma," Susan responded solemnly, and Michael giggled.

"What do I get?"

The now familiar fizzle shot through Susan, and she steeled herself as she turned to face Jason, who was leaning against the fridge, his thumbs hooked in his belt, an amused yet somehow intimate look lighting his eyes. Susan's heart skipped a couple of beats and a host of butterflies unfurled in her midriff as her gaze connected with his. It took considerable effort to keep her voice steady. "You can have a cup of coffee—" she hesitated and glanced at the clock "—and some muffins."

Michael glanced up at her, a glint of mischief in his eyes. "How come you aren't going to ask him if he cleaned up his room and picked up his dirty laundry?"

"Because he's too old to train."

Jason cast her a quick glance, his own eyes glinting, then helped himself to a cup of coffee. Susan put the cake in the oven, then stacked the baking utensils in the sink. Jason half sat on the counter, his legs stretched out in front of him, and every nerve in Susan's body responded to his closeness.

Todd came in and saw Michael painstakingly licking the beater. "Hey, do I get one?"

Susan handed it to him and he went to sit by his brother. He glanced up at his dad, a touch of disgust in his voice. "Susan made us clean our rooms."

Jason tipped his head slightly. "Good for Susan."

"She's going to make us do it every Saturday."

There was a quirk at one corner of the senior Chisholm's mouth. "That's nice."

Realizing he was fighting a lost cause, Todd sighed dramatically and gave his father a woeful look. "She beats us, Dad, and makes us do awful things."

"Fine," his father answered.

Todd grinned and licked a smear of batter off his wrist. "And she took my rubber snake."

Lucy came bouncing into the kitchen, looking sweet and adorable. "My room's done. Can I lick the bowl now?"

Dropping a spoon in it, Susan handed her the bowl. "You be sure to put it in the dishwasher when you're through, okay?" Lucy nodded as she climbed up on a chair.

Patricia had followed Lucy into the kitchen, and Jason indicated her with a nod of his head. "Don't you think you'd better share that with your sister, Lucy?"

Patricia looked at Susan, her expression almost guilty. "No, thanks, Dad. I don't want any."

Jason's eyes narrowed slightly as he studied his elder daughter. Susan interpreted the look as she interjected hurriedly, "There's a dish of fruit left over from breakfast, if you'd rather have that, Trish. It's on the second shelf in the fridge."

He fixed his gaze on her, a contemplative look in his eyes as he took a sip of coffee and watched over the rim of the cup. Susan turned away and started filling the sink with hot water, suspecting he could read her like a book.

As if he decided to let it drop, he shifted his position and looked at his kids, who were all gathered around the table. "So, what have you guys got planned for today?"

Patricia shrugged, then looked at her father. "The boys are going to Reddings', and Susan's going to teach me how to sew." She glanced at Susan, then quickly looked away. "And we're going for a long walk."

"I see," he said softly, as though he really did see. He studied Susan for a moment longer, then looked at Lucy. "And what about you, Luce?"

"Susan's going to make me a new outfit for my Cabbage Patch doll." She pursed her lips and shook her head emphatically. "And we aren't going to bug Grandma or be noisy in the house, because Grandma's really tired." She glanced up at Susan, looking for confirmation. "That's right, isn't it, Susan?"

Susan nodded.

Lucy went on, her face animated with enthusiasm. "And Grandma said I could play with the old curtains in the attic, so I'm going to make a playhouse out in the trees. And have a tea party, maybe."

Jason's eyes were alight with both humor and affection as he watched his small daughter. "The main course being mud pies, no doubt."

Lucy screwed up her face in a guilty expression. "But I won't use Grandma's rolling pin this time, Daddy. I promise. I'll just use the things in the plastic tea set Mikey gave me for Christmas."

Jason's mouth twitched. "That sounds like a good idea."

Lucy gave him another sheepish grimace, then danced out of the room, her curls bobbing. Michael pushed back his chair and stood up. "Hurry up, Todd," he urged. "Dad said we have to pick up the loose papers that blew out of the burning barrel before we can go."

Susan wiped the mixer and put it away, then filled a basket with bran muffins. "Will Len and Duffy be in?"

Jason shook his head. "Not until dinnertime I don't imagine."

Todd put his dirty beater in the dishwasher, helped himself to a muffin and headed for the door. Michael followed him. "We'll be out behind the house if Davy calls, okay?"

Susan acknowledged him with a nod and grimaced slightly as the boys let the back door slam loudly behind them. She poured herself a cup of coffee and carried it and the basket of muffins to the table. Jason followed her and sat down across from her, his expression suddenly sober.

Susan stirred her coffee. "How's Walter?"

Jason sighed and leaned back in his chair. "About the same. It usually takes a while for spells like this to pass."

"Isn't there anything that can be done medically?"

Jason reached for the covered butter dish in the middle of the table. "Yeah, there is. He could have surgery that would relieve the headaches, but he has such a deep-seated fear of both hospitals and doctors, he won't even consider it."

Patricia put her spoon in her empty dish and looked at Susan as she stood up. "I'm going outside, but if you need me for anything, just call me."

"Why don't you give Lucy a hand with her play-house? That way she won't drive the boys crazy."

She nodded and flashed the Chisholm smile. "She drives everybody crazy." She patted her father on the back as she walked past him to put her dish in the sink. "See you later, Daddy."

He watched Patricia leave the kitchen, then with his expression grave, he looked down and absently toyed with his coffee mug. After a moment, he raised his eyes and looked at her. "I know what you're trying to do for her, Susan. She's a good kid, and she deserves a lot more than she gets." He looked away, the muscles in his jaw working, as though he were struggling to maintain a veneer of control. His voice was even more ragged when he continued. "I know her self-image has really suffered this past couple of years, and whether you realize it or not, you've given her the kind of support she needs right now."

Susan's expression became solemn as she gazed at him, her own voice slightly uneven as she tried to lighten his mood. "I was a porker when I was her age so I know how she feels." She smiled halfheartedly as she quietly chastised him. "Peeling carrots and chopping celery is no big deal, Jason. She's the one who has to make the sacrifices."

There was a hint of a smile around his mouth as he raised his head and looked at her. "Is anything a big deal with you?"

She grinned. "Yes. The World Series and mud on a clean kitchen floor."

The laugh lines around his mouth finally creased. "I'll remember that." He sighed and dragged his hand across his face in a weary gesture. "Has Mattie made an appearance since breakfast?"

Susan studied him briefly, then decided to try her hand at a little common-sense counseling. "I know you're worried about her, but I honestly think most of her problem is plain old exhaustion. The rest she's getting is going to make such a difference."

"That's what her doctor says."

Without thinking about it, she reached out and covered his hand in an imploring gesture. "Then listen to him, Jason. And quiet feeling guilty about it. Mattie wouldn't be here if she didn't want to be."

His eyes darkened, and for an instant she thought he was going to turn his hand over and lace his fingers through hers, but he swallowed hard and eased his hand away. His face had a rigid set to it as he said gruffly, "I guess I'd better get moving. I have to go into town for veterinary supplies." Susan watched him go, aching to know what was going on in his mind.

But she never got a chance to find out. From then on, and over the next few days, it was almost as though he were deliberately avoiding her. If he was ignoring her, it would have been different, but he wasn't—he was plainly avoiding her, and that nearly drove her crazy. He'd still get into verbal sparring matches with her at meals, and he had given her another riding lesson, but he always made sure someone was with them, that they didn't spend so much as a minute alone. She'd been raised in a home where everybody's feelings were always out in the open, where people talked about what was bothering them.

Jason Chisholm, however, was not like that. He wasn't about to talk about anything.

Susan tried to convince herself that he wasn't *really* avoiding her, that he was just preoccupied because there was so much work to be done, but she didn't believe that for a minute. And maybe she would have never scraped up the nerve to confront him if it hadn't been for an incident one morning at the breakfast table. It had all started out so innocently.

She was refilling mugs with fresh coffee when Duffy raised his cup and took a sip and tipped his head in approval. "If you ever get hard up you could always auction her off, Jase. Any woman who can make coffee like that should fetch a good price on the open market." He looked utterly pleased with himself, and the others had a chuckle over Duffy's droll little aside.

Susan put her hand on her hip and glared at him, warning him he was treading on dangerous ground.

Jason glanced up at her then solemnly shook his head. "I don't know, Duffy. I don't think she'd train worth a damn."

Susan gave him a slicing look. "Maybe you need a little training yourself."

He grinned at her and gave her a noncommittal shrug. "Maybe."

"Maybe," she said in the same tone of voice, "all of you would like to make your own lunches from now on."

His grin broadened. "I don't think so."

"Then you'd better start treating the cook with a little more respect, or you'll find yourself standing directly behind an apron with a potato peeler in your hand."

The laughter in his eyes held her transfixed as he leaned back in his chair and deliberately baited her. "That's woman's work."

"If you don't quit while you're ahead, Jason Chisholm, you're going to find yourself in very deep trouble," she warned.

The sparkle died and Susan was sure something that closely related to pain flitted across his face. He managed to hold his smile in place as he tore his gaze away. "Yes," he said quietly, "I know."

Susan stared at him, her thoughts tossed into a complete muddle by his response to a seemingly off-hand remark. There was a deeper meaning that she didn't comprehend, but she knew it had something to do with her.

Somehow she managed to get through the next half hour with an outward appearance of normalcy, but mentally she was functioning in a strange disjointed state, almost as though she were caught in a very unsettling dream. She made lunches for the kids, but by the time she hustled them out the door to catch the school bus, she could not even vaguely remember what she'd packed for them.

She'd had to chase after Todd because he'd left his homework lying on the counter, and by the time she returned, the men were leaving the table. Jason was already standing by the door, his hat in his hand, giving the men a list of duties for the day.

With his jaw set in stern lines, he brushed some dried grass off the brim as he spoke to her without making eye contact. "We've got a few chores to do around here, then we'll be pulling out for most of the day. Don't expect us back until around suppertime."

Susan felt oddly inept. "Then you'll want lunches packed."

He finally raised his eyes and looked at her, a soberness there she'd never seen before. "Yeah. If you would. We're trailering the horses over to our leased land, so you can pack everything in the cooler."

She nodded and he put his hat on, then he turned and left the room. The other three followed him out, the screen door slamming loudly behind them.

The silence that remained was cheerless, and Susan set about cleaning up the breakfast dishes and making the men's lunches, her mood glumly introspective. She wasn't stupid. She could read people with the best of them, and she was almost certain that Jason Chisholm was battling with himself, and that a good portion of that battle had something to do with one Susan Lynton. And she didn't like the obvious explanations as to why. She was just finishing wiping off the counters when the door slammed again, and Jason came into the kitchen. Without speaking, he went to the fridge where he kept the veterinary supplies.

He took out a tube of something and stuck it in his pocket, then turned to go. Trying to ignore the fact that the butterflies in her stomach were the size of ostriches, she acted on a wild impulse and confronted him. "Why are you avoiding me, Jase?"

He turned and looked at her, his expression closed. "What makes you think I'm avoiding you?"

Susan gave him the same look she used on the kids when they were trying to pull something over on her. "Because you are."

"I don't know what you're talking about."

"Yes you do. If I get within five feet of you, you bolt like old Riley, and this is the first time in days we've been alone for more than twenty seconds. Is it the perfume I use? Do I have bad breath? Am I contagious or something?"

There was a hint of a smile in his eyes as he said, "Infectious would be a better choice of words."

She was in no mood to be humored by anything cute, and she put her hand on her hip as she glared at him. "I'm not asking you to reveal your bank balance, Jason. All I want to know is why you treat me like a leper."

He spread his legs in a wide stance and hooked his thumbs in his belt. "Maybe," he said in a low, pointed tone, "I avoid you because every time we say more than two words to each other, we end up arguing."

"We aren't arguing," she said hotly. "We're discussing a situation."

"Sounds like arguing."

"God, you're exasperating!"

He grinned and pulled his Stetson low over his eyes. "See you at supper."

He started toward the door and she jumped in front of him, spreading her arms across the open portal. "You aren't getting out of here until you talk to me, Jason Chisholm," she warned. "Damn it, all I want is a simple answer."

"Well, you aren't going to get it."

She could tell by the stubborn set of his jaw and the look in his eyes that she was beating her head against a brick wall. With a sigh of resignation she stuck her hands in her back pockets and looked away. He was about to brush by her when she laid her hand on his arm and he jerked away, almost as though she'd scalded him.

It was an unexpected reaction and she took a long shot. "Jason," she said quietly, "is it because of what happened before...with the kids' mother? Has that turned you off all relationships?"

Suddenly feeling that she had gone too far, she looked down, unable to hold his penetrating gaze. Lord, but she had got in over her head *this* time, she thought wildly as she felt unexpected tears burn her eyes. What a stupid thing to say.

She heard him draw in a deep breath, then with infinite gentleness, Jase hooked his knuckles under her chin and forced her head up. There was a different kind of solemnness in his eyes as he met her gaze with heart-stopping directness. "It has nothing to do with Eileen, Susan," he said very quietly. "Whatever wounds were inflicted then have healed long ago."

There was so much emotion unfolding inside her that Susan could barely breathe as she whispered, "Then what is it, Jase? I need to know."

For the longest time he simply looked at her, his eyes giving nothing away. But she sensed a deep discontentment about him, as if he were enduring some inner struggle. And she couldn't stand that. Reaching up she touched his face, her voice breaking as she said, "Something's happening between us, and I'm getting in so far over my head, I don't know what to do. Without even trying, you landed this on me and I can't even fight back."

He shut his eyes in a grimace as he pulled her hand away. "Sue," he whispered raggedly. "God, Sue... don't."

"Talk to me, Jase," she pleaded. "I'm not asking for much. I just want you to talk to me."

He opened his eyes, eyes that were dark and smoky, and as if drawn against his will, he cupped her face in his callused hands and softly stroked her cheeks with his thumbs. "Just because you're attracted doesn't mean it's anything more, Susan. It doesn't mean those feelings are real."

Who's he trying to kid? she thought, her senses thrown into a mindless muddle by the feeling of his hands on her face. *This is as real as anything is ever going to get.* But for once, she didn't argue. Not now, not while he was looking at her the way he was. She had a nearly uncontrollable urge to step into his arms, but even in the daze she was in, she knew that Jason Chisholm would withdraw the minute she did. As much as she loathed to do it, she knew she had to put some distance between them. And somehow she had to get him talking.

"Then it's not just me, is it? It's happening to you, too." There was a flash of something in his eyes that resembled anguish, and it aroused such a fierce protectiveness in her she had to fight to keep from responding.

There was a quiet, almost desperate seriousness about him as he slowly stroked her lips with his thumb. "Yes, it's happening to me, too."

"Then why—"

He pressed his thumb firmly against her mouth to silence her. "I'm old enough to be your father, Susan."

"You aren't."

She could see the faintest glimmer of amusement in his eyes as he said firmly, "Yes, I am."

That small exchange helped to break the tension, and Susan pressed the issue, knowing that by doing so they were steering away from dangerous ground. "You are not."

The glimmer intensified and he said warningly, "Susan—"

"Well, then, you must have been a very precocious teenager."

He grinned and let his hand slip to her shoulder. "My teenage years have nothing to do with it. I'm forty-four years old. I was *seventeen* when you were born, for Pete's sake. I'm telling you, I'm old enough to be your father."

She lifted her chin in a gesture that was unmitigated defiance as she said slowly and very distinctly, "But you *aren't* my father."

His grin deepened. "Thank God."

She narrowed her eyes, but before she could respond, he patted her on the cheek as if she were Lucy's age, then eased past her. "I'll see you at supper," he repeated as he brushed by.

The screen door slammed behind him, and she could hear the sound of his footsteps fading as he headed toward the barn. Her knees refused to support her one moment longer and she numbly sank to the floor, her back braced against the doorjamb. She was hot and cold, and she felt as though she had just stepped off some hair-raising ride at a fair.

Closing her eyes, she tipped her head back and weakly rested it against the wall, waiting for her pulse to return to normal. But the recollection of the galvanizing sensation of his hands on her face did incredible things to her heart rate, and she clenched her fists against the warmth that pumped through her. If he could turn her into such a wreck with a single touch, she wondered what kind of state she'd be in if things ever really got out of hand between them. It would be so unbelievable....

There was a feather-light touch against her temple, and with a massive effort she opened her eyes. Jason was crouched beside her, his hazel eyes glinting green, his expression softened by a heart-stopping tenderness. With infinite gentleness he rested his knuckles against her jaw and slowly smoothed his thumb across her cheek, an irresistible half smile pulling at his mouth. "Don't tell me I finally won a round," he said, his voice low and husky.

Feeling as though her whole body were paralyzed by the magic of his touch, Susan gazed up at him, her expression soft and misty. "You fight dirty, Jason Chisholm," she whispered unevenly.

Very lightly he drew his thumb across her bottom lip. "So do you."

"I don't."

The dimple appeared. "I knew you were trouble the minute I laid eyes on you."

Susan drew a shaky breath, then spoke, her voice still unsteady. "You were only guessing."

He slowly shook his head, his eyes darkening as his expression sobered. "No, I knew."

Susan felt drugged by the intensity that enveloped them, almost afraid to breathe for fear she would shatter the spell that bound them. He continued to caress her face and she closed her eyes, losing all sense of space and time beneath the mesmerizing effect of his touch. Finally opening her eyes, she moistened her lips and was about to speak.

Once again Jason touched his thumb to her mouth, his hand curving against her jaw, his fingers caressing the soft skin of her neck. "Don't, Susan," he whispered, his voice ragged. "It's so damned hard to keep things in perspective right now, and I have to."

She pressed her face against his hand, her eyes as readable as a book. "Why?"

He inhaled sharply, his eyes sliding to her mouth. He clenched his jaw then swallowed. "Because I'm a generation older than you. It's as simple as that."

Susan was experiencing so much right then that she could barely speak, but somehow she managed an unsteady smile. "That's your opinion. Maybe you're just too cagey to be caught."

The lopsided grin appeared. "There's an old saying about fools rushing in where wise men fear to tread. And under the circumstances, I think I'd better rely on wisdom."

She smiled at him softly, her eyes luminous. An unspoken harmony seemed to radiate between them, and that feeling of intimate companionship was so powerful it was almost as if they were physically bound together.

Jason sighed as he molded his hand against her jaw, and she covered it with her own. "I don't suppose you'd hold me right now, would you?" she whispered unsteadily.

She caught a flash of laughter in his eyes before his voice dropped warningly. "No."

"Could we discuss it?"

He finally laughed aloud, his hands slipping threateningly to her neck. "Lord, but you're impossible."

"I'm a determined woman," she said, half laughing, half serious.

"So I've discovered."

Her expression changed, her gaze becoming intent. "Jason—"

He firmly shook his head. "No, Susan. We are not going to talk about it."

She stared at him a moment, then decided on a different tack. "Why did you come back?"

"I saw Breezy hanging around the corral and I thought she was looking a little bored. So I thought the two of you might like to come with us."

She stared at him a split second longer, then her eyes lit up. "Are you serious?"

Smiling, he gently smoothed back a loose curl as he nodded. "Yes."

Her face grew sober. "Do you want me to come, or are you asking me out of some warped sense of duty?"

His voice was very husky. "I want you to come."

For some insane reason Susan found herself fighting tears and she blinked rapidly, trying to hold back the intense feelings that were growing in her.

Turning his hand beneath hers, he laced his fingers through hers and stood up. "Come on," he said quietly as he pulled her to her feet. "Let's get moving before this gets out of hand."

He didn't release his hold on her immediately, and there was something deeply reassuring about that physical link. He gazed at her a moment longer then let her go, a gleam in his eyes. "Well, woman, you'd better jump to it."

With her feeling of well-being soaring, she grinned at him. "And you know where and how high you can jump."

He grinned back at her as he pulled his hat low over his eyes. "That's what I like about you, Susan. You're so servile and obedient."

She made a face at him and he tapped her firmly under the chin, then turned to go. Susan suddenly remembered Mattie and Walter, and her high spirits took a nosedive. Exhaling sharply, she suppressed a sharp pang of regret. "I can't go. What about lunch for Mattie and Walter?"

He shrugged off her concern. "Walter can manage. I'll go tell Mattie you're coming with me, and I'll catch Walter on the way to the barn." He checked the pocket of his jean jacket for the tube he'd taken out of the fridge, then started toward the door. "How much time do you need to get ready?"

"Ten minutes. Your lunches are ready to go. I just have to pack the cooler."

He looked at her from beneath his hat brim, a smile tugging at his mouth. "Don't you think you'd better pack something for yourself? It's going to be a long day."

She laughed and gave him a wave of dismissal. "I'll eat grass."

He was still grinning as he went out the door. "You'll have to fight off a herd of cows to get to it."

Susan flew into action the minute the screen door slammed. By the time the men pulled up by the back door, she'd taken a pot of tea and some toast up to

Mattie, packed the lunch in the cooler, filled a huge thermos and changed into a long-sleeve shirt.

She was carrying the large Styrofoam cooler into the porch when Jason came in with a pair of cowboy boots and a hat. "Here, you'd better put these on."

Susan set the cooler on the floor and took the gear Jason handed her. "Did you find Walter?"

"Yeah. He said he'd come in and check on Mattie." Jason picked up the cooler and turned toward the door. "What have you got in here—bricks?"

Laughing, she twisted her hair on top of her head and covered it with the straw Stetson. "That and some grass."

He gave her a sharp look as he hit the latch on the door with his elbow. "Not funny, Susan."

She kicked off her runners and pulled on the boots, then picking up the huge thermos and a light jacket, she dashed out the door behind him. The truck was parked by the hedge, the sounds of horses and creaking saddles coming from the blue-and-silver six-horse trailer hitched on behind.

Jason placed the cooler in the back of the vehicle, and Susan set the thermos beside it. Len was stretched out in the back on a pile of hay, his hat tipped over his eyes, his hands laced behind his head, idly chewing on a piece of straw. She laughed and caught the toe of his boot and gave it a shake. "What's the matter, Len? Won't they let you ride in the front with the big boys?"

He peeked out from beneath his hat and woefully shook is head. "I had a rough night last night, Susan. A rough night."

Duffy's drawl came from the cab. "You should quit your tomcatting around if you can't handle it." He chuckled. "Don't go in the kitchen, boy, if you can't handle the heat."

"Someday I'm gonna punch your lights out, Duff," Len responded mildly. "Sure as hell, I am."

Shaking his head in amusement, Jason opened the door on the driver's side and Susan stepped in and slid past the wheel. Duffy moved over to make room for her, then draped his arm across the back of the seat and grinned. "I hope you brought a sticky saddle for her, Jase. Remember the last time ol' Clayton brought one of them eastern dudes out here? We jest about had to tie him on a horse. Every time that old cow pony'd make a turn, he'd slide out of the saddle neater'n a whistle."

Susan gave him a sardonic look. "Who did you give him to ride, old Riley?"

Duffy chuckled and stuck a toothpick in his mouth. "Hell, no. We put him on Breezy. She got so fed up with him that she finally laid down on him. It was funnier 'n hell."

Jason was grinning when Susan glanced at him for confirmation. Putting the truck in gear, he slowly pulled away, verifying Duffy's tale with a nod. "It was pretty bad, all right. I'd wanted Len to take him out in the truck, but Clayton was sure he could manage. And the guy insisted that the only way he could form any realistic concepts about ranching was to ride." He laughed and shook his head as he glanced at Duffy. "You don't need to worry this time, Duff. Susan has a better defined anchorage than he had."

Duffy chuckled. "Yep, with them long legs of hers, she'll stick on that horse jest like one of them old clothes pegs."

"Look, Duffy," Susan said firmly, "if you're nice to me today, I won't give you the piece of cherry pie with all the pits in it at lunch."

Folding his hands across his chest, he slouched in the seat and chuckled again. "Sounds fair."

As it turned out, Susan was the one who got the piece with all the cherry stones in it, much to the delight of the three men. But by then she was flying so high, she could have eaten a whole gravel pit, and done it with a smile on her face. It had been a wonderful morning, and she reveled in every second of it.

They had decided to eat the noontime meal overlooking a shallow stream on a grassy slope purple with crocuses. Off in the distance, cattle dotted the rolling hills. Len had taken the horses down to water them as Susan watched, silently wishing she had brought her camera.

Jason was stretched out on a horse blanket he'd taken from the trailer, his hands laced behind his head as he watched the clouds. Susan was sitting cross-legged beside him, relishing the wind, the sun on her back, and the rich smell of spring. Duffy was seated on the ground with his back propped against a rocky outcrop, rolling a cigarette, a cup of steaming coffee propped between his knees.

Susan reached out and raked her fingers through the dry grass. The ground was dust dry and there were very few spikes of green amid the brown. She glanced at Jason. "How bad is it?"

He rolled onto his side, then put on his hat and reached for the thermos. "Bad enough. It takes more than one season for this land to recover and even longer if it's overgrazed, and this is the third year in a row we've had practically no rain. We may have to reduce the size of herd this year, but with careful range management, we'll be okay." His expression grew sober. "There'll be a few who won't be so lucky, though."

Duffy chuckled. "If it don't rain soon, we're going to spend the whole damned summer shuffling cattle from one pasture to another. We'll put in more miles than a traveling salesman."

Susan grinned and looked back at Jason. "Clayton said the Double Diamond covers a little more than thirty thousand acres. With that much land, why would you have to cut your herd?"

"We normally run about a thousand head of cattle, but if you want to manage the range effectively, you need about twenty-two acres per cow-calf unit. And when it gets bad like this, you need considerably more—maybe even double that. And the condition of our range is always our primary concern."

"Clayton says you lease land."

"About a quarter of the acreage is crown land leased from the government. The rest is deeded—most of it's been in the Chisholm family for years."

Len came up the hill leading the four horses, and pushing his hat to the back of his head, he dropped the reins and came toward them. "I seen that old blue cow down by the willow thicket with two calves in tow. That must be the fifth year in a row she's had twins.

If she keeps that up, she could make you a rich man, Jase.''

Susan's expression was one of amazement. ''A thousand head of cows, and you know the performance of *one*?''

Jason laughed and stood up. ''Some are more memorable than others.''

Duffy sighed wistfully. ''Sort of applies to females in general, don't it?''

Len slapped his thigh and let out a loud guffaw and Susan, realizing she was faced with an incurable situation, shook her head. ''You guys are really hopeless, do you know that?''

Still grinning, Len challenged her. ''Now that ain't so, Susan. We've always got hope.''

That brought a snort of amusement from Duffy, and Jason warned, ''You'd better quit while you're ahead.''

She gave him a rueful look. ''I think you're right.''

Len had looped the reins over his horse's neck and, without using a stirrup, caught the horn and swung effortlessly into the saddle. Susan watched, awestruck. ''I'd give my right arm to learn how to do that.''

''Aw, hell. That's easy,'' Duffy offered as he picked up his reins. ''There's a little trick to it. Here. Watch.''

He repeated the process for her, and Susan watched intently, then shook her head as he settled himself in the saddle. ''Never, never in a thousand years could I manage that. You have to be part gymnast to do that.''

''Get ol' Jase to show you how. He can get on from both sides, and hell, there was one time we made a few bucks on him. Remember, Jase? It was roundup at the

Flying U and ol' Tyler said you couldn't do it at a gallop, and you said you could. So we ran that mean-mouthed half-broke gelding past you, and you caught that horn and was in that saddle before Tyler could blink. Ol' Tyler jest stood there dumb like, not believin' what he was seein'. Hell, we had a good laugh over that."

Susan looked at Jason. He was busily prodding a clump of grass with his toe, and she could swear his neck was turning red as he tried to shrug it off. "It was nothing more than a stupid stunt." He finally glanced up and gave her a sheepish lopsided grin. "And I damned near ripped my arm off doing it."

Susan laughed, delighted that there still was some boy left in the man. "Sounds like the kind of thing that legends are made of."

Len stroked his chin and chuckled. "It's a good thing ol' Tyler's a few years younger 'n you, Jase. I figure you two would have done some serious hell-raising if you'd been twenty at the same time."

Jason had held Susan's horse while she mounted, and laughed as he handed her the reins. "Tyler did just fine all by himself."

By the unmitigated Chisholm charm and the glint of devilry in his eyes, Susan strongly suspected the same could be said for Jason Chisholm.

CHAPTER SIX

THE PHONE RANG, and Susan closed the dishwasher door, set the switch, then turned to answer it. The muscles in her thighs protested with every movement, and she groaned, knowing she was certainly paying the price for the day she'd spent riding with Jase. Drying her hands on the towel she had draped over her shoulder, she cradled the receiver against her shoulder. "Double Diamond Ranch."

A man answered. "Hello. Could I speak to Mr. Chisholm, please?"

Susan glanced at the clock on the stove. "He won't be home for another hour or so. Could I take a message?"

"Is Mrs. Chisholm available?"

"I'm afraid Mrs. Chisholm can't come to the phone. She's resting right now."

There was a pause, and Susan sensed a thread of urgency in his voice when he finally spoke. "Is there any way you could get word to Mr. Chisholm?"

"Yes, if necessary." Something—a certain timbre in the man's voice—got to her and she caught herself frowning. "Is something wrong?"

"Yes, I'm afraid there is. This is Mr. Carter. I'm the principal of the school Michael and Todd attend. We've had a—a freak accident."

Alarm shot through her. "What happened?"

She could sense him considering how much to tell her. "The classes were dismissed for recess when a thunderstorm hit." There was a frightening pause before he explained. "Lightning struck in the playground."

Her alarm escalated to fear, and Susan could barely breathe. "Who?" It was all she could say.

As if realizing what grim thoughts she was thinking, Mr. Carter hastened to explain. "No one was actually...was critically injured." The way he said it sent a cold shiver down her spine. She forced herself to stay calm as he continued. "Seven students and one teacher were close to the spot where it struck, and they were all badly shaken up. Michael was one." The principal was obviously skirting the seriousness of the situation, but at least Michael was still... She couldn't even think about what *could* have happened to him.

She forced herself to concentrate on what Mr. Carter was saying. "It would take too long to get ambulances out, so we've arranged for private transportation to take them to the hospital in High River. The district nurse will be with them."

With her fear neutralized by the need to act, Susan's mind finally clicked into gear. Walter had taken her car apart that morning, Len had taken the Suburban to town for parts, and there wasn't another vehicle on the place. She wasn't even sure where Jase was. And she didn't have a clue how long it would take her to track him down. And someone had to be at that hospital for Michael. How? Who? A new thought cut into her frantic thoughts. Wherever Michael was,

Davy wouldn't be far away. "By any chance, is David Redding another one who was hurt?"

"Yes, but I haven't been able to reach his parents—there's no answer." For the first time, the professional cool of the principal gave way and he sounded extremely agitated.

But Susan didn't allow herself to think about that. They were wasting time. "I'll contact the Reddings." She knew Carol was home; she'd stopped in less than an hour ago for coffee. Susan's mind raced. They'd never be able to get to the school before the makeshift ambulance left; it would make more sense if she and Carol headed right for the hospital. If they drove like hell, they might even be able to beat them there. "Tell Michael and Davy we'll meet them at the hospital."

"I'll tell them. And you're going to contact David's parents," he said, making certain the directions were clear.

"Yes."

"Fine then. We'll see you at the hospital."

Susan hung up the phone and pressed her shaking hands tightly against her thighs as she groped for the right words to tell Carol what had happened. Taking a deep breath to steady the awful churning in her stomach, she dialed the number. One ring. Two. Three. Susan whispered urgently, "Come on, Carol. Answer the damned phone." Seven. Eight. Nine.

"Hello!" an irritated voice answered.

"Hi, Carol. It's Susan."

There was a groan, then a laugh. "Your ears must be burning. I called you every name in the book for dragging me in from the garden."

Susan's voice was surprisingly steady as she said quietly, "There's been an accident at school, Carol." Then, calmly, she told Davy's mother what had happened.

Carol's voice showed signs of stress when she said, "Is everyone okay?"

"Mr. Carter said no one was critically injured, but you could tell he was pretty worried."

"I'll leave right now."

Susan glanced at the clock and wiped her hand on her jeans. "Carol, could you pick me up? I don't have a clue where Jase is, and I don't know how to track him down. And somebody has to be there with Mike."

"Just a minute." Susan could hear muffled conversation, and she paced back and forth as far as the cord would allow, chewing worriedly on her lip.

"Derek just came in. He's going after Jase, and I'll pick you up in five minutes—no, ten. I have to put some slacks on."

"I'm going to tell Walter what happened so he can keep an eye on Mattie, then I'll go out to the road and meet you there."

"What are you going to tell Mattie?"

"Not the truth, that's for certain. At least not until I find out how he is."

"I think that's wisest." There was a pause, then Carol continued, her voice sounding oddly hollow. "I'll be there as soon as I can."

Susan hung up the phone and raced out the door into the porch, letting the screen door crash shut behind her as she flew down the stairs. She found Walter puttering in the garage. Once again she related the story. "I need you to stay in the house, Walter, in case

Mattie needs anything." She rested her hand on his arm, her face marked by anxiety. "But you mustn't tell her what's happened. I'm not going to wake her, so when she does get up, you just tell her that I went to town with Carol to pick up some things, okay?"

Walter nodded and methodically wiped his greasy hands on a rag. "I'll watch her," he said with painstaking slowness. "You go to Mikey." He picked up a small tool kit and started toward the house. "I'll fix the basement door. Then she won't wonder why I'm inside."

Susan didn't have the time to waste, but nevertheless, she put her arms around him and hugged him. "God bless you, Walter. I'd have never thought of that."

He patted her awkwardly and smiled in encouragement. "You go to Mikey."

And Susan went. She dashed into the porch, through the kitchen and into her room, stripping off her blouse on her way. She grabbed a clean shirt from the closet, thrust her arms into it, snatched her shoulder bag and raced out the door, buttoning up the front of her blouse as she went. She hit the driveway at a dead run, and for the first time since she got the phone call, she couldn't block out thoughts of what she might be facing at the hospital. *Please, God,* she prayed silently, *let him be all right. Let them all be okay.* Thunder rolled overhead, rumbling down the valley and fading off in the distance. She was breathing hard and her body was damp with perspiration by the time she reached the main road, and she found it hard to catch her breath in the clammy, still heat. She had started down the road toward the Reddings' when she finally saw the plume of dust approaching. The vehicle hadn't rolled to a stop before Susan had the passenger door open. Carol braked sharply then rested her head on the steering wheel. "You're going to have to drive, Sue," she said unevenly. "I'm shaking so bad, I can't."

Susan didn't argue. She went around the car and slid behind the wheel, slammed the door and put it in gear. It was a big old Buick that responded with a throaty reverberation of power and a hail of gravel as she tramped the accelerator. There were enough horses under the hood to make this thing move, she thought grimly, and she was going to use every one of them.

She glanced at Carol. "Does speed bother you?"

"No."

"I don't know the road that well so you're going to have to tell me where the rough breaks and the curves are."

"Okay." There was a brief silence, then Carol said with a quiet kind of dread, "I've got this awful feeling in my stomach."

Susan's worried frown deepened and she gripped the wheel tighter. "I know. So have I."

Susan pushed the big car to its limit, and the miles flashed by. The only time either of them spoke was when Carol voiced a caution and Susan acknowledged it. By the time they pulled into the parking lot at the hospital, they were both tight-lipped and pale.

And then they had to wait.

The hospital had been notified about the incoming injuries and as edgy as she was, Susan was aware of the state of readiness, and it didn't help to know that two additional doctors had been called in from their offices. Knowing that made it all the more frightening; it was as if they were preparing for the worst.

When word came that the casualties were being unloaded, Carol and Susan exchanged one long anxious look then followed the nurse. The first stretcher they brought in was totally shrouded, and through the tunnel vision of her own fear, Susan saw Carol go deathly white as she mouthed something, then her knees started to buckle beneath her. But Susan moved quickly, managing to catch the woman before she went down. Susan felt a horrible chill slithering through her; she, too, recognized the battered running shoes that showed beneath the blanket. They were David's.

A man in a crumpled shirt pushed through the medical staff and hurried over to them. "Mrs. Redding, it's not what you think," he said frantically. "He's not—his face was burned and we're concerned about his eyes. The nurse didn't want them exposed to light until the doctor has a chance to examine him."

Carol closed her eyes and hauled in a deep breath. "Oh, God, I thought he was—"

"Mom, is that you?" came a scared little voice from beneath the sheet.

Carol drew in another shaky breath, then visibly steeling herself, she went over to the stretcher and grasped the small, grubby hand that had wormed its way out. Her voice was calm and reassuring as she took it in both of hers. "Yes, honey. I'm right here."

"My eyes hurt."

Her steadiness wavered slightly as she said, "I know, sweetheart." Just then an attendant grasped the gurney to wheel it into another room. Still holding the boy's hand, Carol followed, speaking quietly to her son.

Susan turned away, her heart in her throat. Finally she spotted Michael. He was chalk white with a definite redness down one side of his face. There were streaks of blood under his nose and down his T-shirt, and his pupils were so dilated his eyes appeared to be black. He looked so scared. She didn't really give a damn about "procedure," and she didn't really give a damn about the vexed look the nurse gave her. All she cared about was giving that child some measure of comfort. Overpowered by an overwhelming relief that made her feel shaky, she pushed her way through some empty stretchers to get to him. She didn't dare speak as she slipped her arms around him and held him close against her.

He wound his arms around her neck in a strangling hold and managed to choke out her name. "Susan..."

"Shh, love. It's okay. Everything's going to be okay."

"I thought Davy was dead after."

Susan had to wait a moment before she dared answer him. "But he's not, Michael. His mom's with him right now, and the doctor's checking him."

She felt him tremble, as though he was trying hard not to cry. "He can't see. Is he going to be blind?"

Gently bracketing his face in her hands, she tried to think of an honest comparison, to give him something familiar to relate to. "You know how your dad always makes you kids stay away when he's welding because it can hurt your eyes?"

Dragging his hand across his face, Michael nodded.

"A flash of lightning that close would be the same. If he wasn't looking right at it, maybe David will just have really sore eyes for a while." She gently smoothed his hair as she smiled at him with reassurance. "They'll take good care of him here, love, so try not to worry."

He slipped his hand into hers and hung on for dear life. "Where's Dad?"

"Mr. Redding has gone to get him. They should be here soon."

He looked away, and she could see tears along his lashes as his grip became almost painfully tight. "I'm glad you're here, Susan. I was so scared."

It was a tough battle to keep her smile in place, but somehow she managed it. "I'm glad I'm here, too." Her expression was filled with compassion as she studied his profile. "Do you want to tell me about it, Michael?"

He turned his head and looked at her, his pale face very solemn. "It was so freaky. We were out playing soccer at recess and a big thunderstorm came in really fast. Miss McDougal came to get us in, then wham. There was this awful crash and the next thing I knew, we were all down on the ground."

He was beginning to warm to the retelling of the drama, and an amused, knowing look kindled in Susan's eyes. Once he got over the shock and the fear, Mike would revel in this. He wiped his nose then continued. "Everybody started to get up, and they were all acting really dopey like, but Davy didn't move. Then Miss McDougal crawled over to him. You know, we couldn't find her shoes, then Mark found them by the backstop. That lightning must have blew them right off her feet. And my nose was bleeding and—'' He swallowed as he became even paler. "I'm going to be sick, Susan."

There was a stainless-steel basin on one of the stretchers and Susan grabbed it, and grasping Michael around the shoulders, she raised him up as he started retching. His nose started to bleed again, and suddenly there was a crowd of medical people around him. One doctor started snapping out orders. Susan held the boy securely against her and kept talking to him in a soothing tone of voice. "It's okay, love. It's okay." The bout of sickness passed and she glanced at the doctor, knowing what he was bound to be thinking. She quietly explained, "He's prone to bad nose-bleeds, Doctor."

The doctor acknowledged the information with a nod, then smiled down at Michael. "Okay, son. Let's get you into an examining room and have a look."

Susan was just about to enter the room when Carol came half running down the corridor toward her, her face drawn. "They're sending Davy to Calgary, Susan. The doctor here wants to have a specialist look at his eyes."

For a moment, Susan thought *she* was going to be sick, but seeing the stricken look on her face, Carol quickly explained. "They don't think there's any permanent damage—more of a temporary trauma—but they want to be on the safe side." She managed a weak grin. "It isn't every day they get a kid in who's seen lightning strike."

"You aren't driving, are you?"

"No, I'm going in the ambulance with David. When Derek comes, tell him they're sending him to the Calgary General."

"Sure. Are you leaving right now?"

"As soon as they finish bandaging his eyes." She took a deep breath. "How's Mikey?"

Susan absently wiped blood from her hands as she gave a worried shrug. "He's been sick to his stomach and his damned nose keeps bleeding—and he's shaken up, but I think he's all right. The doctor's checking him over now."

"They're ready to go, Mrs. Redding," called a nurse.

Carol squeezed Susan's arm as she turned away. "I'll give you a call as soon as I can, Sue." She stopped and dug the car keys out of her purse and shoved them into Susan's hand. "Here. I'll leave these with you. You might need the car."

Susan nodded, then gave her a quick hug and whispered shakily, "I don't care if it's four in the morning—just let us know."

"I will."

It was well over an hour later when Derek and Jase finally arrived. Susan had called the Double Diamond and was pacing up and down the hallway outside of X ray, her arms folded rigidly across her breasts as she nervously chewed her lip. The doctor's examination had turned up a nasty swelling on the back of Michael's head, and they were now x-raying his skull. She looked up to see the two men striding down the corridor toward her, both of them with anxious looks on their faces.

Somehow she managed to glue a smile on her face as she went to meet them. She never gave them a chance to speak. "They're both fine." She took one look at Jase's face and she wanted to cry, but she made the smile stick and tried to keep her voice steady. "They were both shaken up, but there's nothing seriously—"

"Where's Davy and Carol?" Derek interrupted, his concern making him agitated and abrupt.

Susan took a deep breath. How could she tell him without scaring him half to death? But she told him. And he listened with far more composure than she expected. But the whole time she was explaining about the freak accident and what had happened, she was acutely aware of Jase standing beside her, his whole body stiff as he stared blindly down the corridor. If it wasn't for the way he had his jaw clenched and the haggard look on his face, she would have wondered if he was even listening to her. *Like a rock,* she thought, as an intolerable ache started to unfold in her chest.

She could cope with almost anything, but she couldn't stand to see him endure one crisis after another with such rigid stoicism.

Derek jerked her back from her solemn thoughts. "When did the ambulance leave?"

"A little more than an hour ago."

"I'm heading off now. I'll make up some time on the road."

Susan dug the keys from the back pocket of her jeans. "Carol left me the keys to your car. Will you need it?"

He took the keys from her. "Yeah. We came in Jase's truck."

"You need gas, Derek. There's less than a quarter of a tank."

"Right." He caught Jason by the shoulder. "We'll talk to you later, Jase. Tell Michael we're thinking about him."

Jason only nodded and raised his hand in a silent farewell as Derek turned to leave. He stonily watched his neighbor walk down the corridor, and it wasn't until Derek disappeared from view that he finally spoke. "How long has Michael been in X ray?"

His voice was devoid of emotion, and Susan avoided looking at him as she answered, "They took him in just before you came." She motioned toward a small sitting area a short distance down the corridor. "Why don't we sit in there. I imagine he'll be a while yet."

Wordlessly Jason followed her and sat down beside her on the small settee. Resting his arms across his thighs, he hunched forward, his hands clasped between his knees as he stared at the floor. The lines around his mouth were deeply defined by anxiety and he looked so tired and so worried that Susan couldn't stand it any longer. She forced her hand between both of his.

He didn't look at her, but she heard him draw in a ragged breath as he finally relaxed a little, and pressing palm against palm, carefully laced his fingers through hers. He tried to speak, then stopped and swallowed heavily before he finally whispered, "Thank God you were here, Susan. Knowing you were here...that he wasn't alone—" His voice broke, and he abruptly looked away. Fighting her own battle, Susan simply tightened her hold on his hand.

Several minutes passed before he leaned back, and resting his head against the wall, he finally looked at her. "Is he really okay?"

"He has an awful lump on his head and I think he has a bit of a flash burn on his face, but other than that, he seems to be fine." She smiled at him and gave his hand a little shake. "You know Michael. This is going to be the highlight of the school year for him— something that broke up the tedium. It'll be one of his adventures, and you know damned well he'll milk it for all it's worth."

Jason's eyes finally lost that bleak look as he gave her a warped smile. "Do you mean I'm going to hear about it a few hundred times?"

"Mr. and Mrs. Chisholm?" A nurse had appeared. Jase gave Susan an intent look, but she only grinned and shrugged. Her grin deepened even more when he acknowledged the nurse without bothering to correct her mistake, then continued to hold Susan's hand as they stood up.

"They've taken Michael to a room. You can wait with him until the doctor has a chance to talk to you." She started down the corridor. "If you'll come with me, I'll take you to him."

"How is he?" Jason asked, unconsciously tightening his grip on Susan's hand.

The nurse smoothly sidestepped the question with an ease born from experience. "The doctor will be with you shortly and he'll be able to answer all your questions."

They found Michael sitting up in bed, a disgruntled look on his face. "They made me pee in a bottle," he said with disgust.

Susan managed not to laugh. "That's one of life's little curve balls, Mike."

"That's not funny, Susan."

"I'm not laughing."

He gave her an accusing look. "Inside you are." Then he looked at his dad and said brightly, "Hi, Dad. Did Susan tell you it blew Miss McDougal's shoes off? And the doctor says Davy's going to be okay, it just scorched him a little. And did Susan tell you I barfed out there?" he said, waving vaguely at the door.

Susan could see the anxiety literally drain out of Jase, and he sat down rather suddenly on the edge of the bed, his hand still gripping hers. "How are you feeling?"

"Fine," Michael answered airily. "I've got a headache, but the doctor says that's because it looks like somebody hit me on the back of the head with a baseball bat. But I don't know how because I was flat out on my stomach when I woke up. How could I have a lump on the back of my head, Dad?"

"Maybe," his dad offered with a hint of a grin, "it was one of Miss McDougal's shoes."

"Do you 'spose?" Mike asked wide-eyed. "Hey, that's right on." He gingerly touched the back of his head. "The doctor says I have to stay in the hospital tonight so they can keep me under obser...ob-surd..."

"Observation," Susan supplied with an amused smile.

"What does that mean?"

"It means they're going to watch you."

"Watch me do what?" he asked, suddenly suspicious.

"We're going to watch you sleep, young man," said the doctor as he came into the room. He directed his attention to Jason and Susan. "He has a slight concussion, so I'd like to keep him overnight. The principal was very definite about us not taking any chances." The physician turned to face Michael, a kindly smile on his face. "We have some supper here for you. So why don't you let your mom and dad head home to theirs, and they can come get you first thing in the morning."

Michael didn't move a muscle. It was as though he were digesting the entire concept of what the doctor's comment suggested. Susan could feel a flush creeping up her face and she opened her mouth to explain, but with a wicked grin, Michael smoothly intercepted her clarification. "That works for me," he said, mimicking one of the catch phrases of a favorite TV star. With perfectly contrived innocence, he turned to Susan and his father. "Why don't you guys go home and I'll see you in the morning."

Susan could have strangled him. She knew that look; he was up to something. But he never gave his game away until she bent over to kiss him goodbye. He gave her a big hug, then in a voice loud enough for his father, the doctor and half of the hospital to hear, he said, "Good night, Mom." She saw Jase's mouth twitch and she thought she detected a hint of humor in his eyes, but he acted as though he hadn't heard.

The minute they stepped out of the room, Susan could feel Jason withdraw into himself, and they walked in total silence to the truck. Susan was dumbfounded to see how low the sun was on the horizon. It didn't seem as if she had been at the hospital that long, but when she glanced at her watch, she realized it was well after seven o'clock.

As they approached the vehicle, Jason fished the keys out of his shirt pocket. Without looking at her, he said, "Do you mind driving?"

She cast a troubled glance at him as she reached out her hand. "No, I don't mind." She couldn't see his face that clearly, but she sensed he was suddenly exhausted beyond words.

How does he manage all this on his own, she thought soberly as she climbed behind the wheel. *He's faced with a severe drought, he has a mother who is definitely not well, he's trying to raise four kids without their mother, and he has at least eight people dependent on him for their welfare. And today he came within a hairbreadth of losing a son.*

As she started the vehicle, she glanced across the cab at him. He was slouched in the seat with his head back and his eyes closed. He wouldn't sleep; he was simply shutting himself off. This way he wouldn't leave himself open, he wouldn't have to talk. And Susan was torn between wanting to shake him and wanting to stop the truck and simply hold him. But she did neither. She drove home, the mugginess pressing down on her like a wet blanket. Ahead of her, against the jagged outline of the mountains, the water-laden thunderclouds rolled up against the peaks in dark banks, trapped against the rocky barrier, unable to move east to the dry land. And to the north, she could hear thunder rolling across the heavens. There would be no rain tonight.

Once they reached the Double Diamond, Jason went directly upstairs to see Mattie. Susan dealt with the kids, assuring them that Michael was really fine, and that he would be home tomorrow. Walter had remained in the house and between him and Tricia, they had made supper. Susan opened the cupboard to get the filters for the coffeepot, then checked the other cupboard doors. Every hinge had been oiled and tightened, and the loose handles had all been fixed. She'd bet the farm that there wasn't a loose screw, a squeaky hinge, a burned out light bulb or a dripping faucet in the whole place. When she experimentally opened and closed the cupboard drawer that used to stick, she realized that Walter was quietly watching her inspection. She grinned at him. "Apple pies for you tomorrow, Walter."

He gave her a sly smile. "Tomorrow I fix your car."

Susan caught his drift and holding up her hands in surrender, she laughed. "Okay, okay—you made your point. Apple pie *and* Yorkshire pudding." Chuckling to himself and nodding in approval, Walter picked up his tool kit and shuffled out.

She was still smiling to herself when she turned around, and her stomach did a funny little lurch. Jase was standing at the dining-room archway with his hands stuck in the back pockets of his jeans, his shoulder braced against the framework. He was watching her with a steady, unnerving look.

She felt oddly uncomfortable, as though he'd caught her doing something he disapproved of, and it was all she could do to keep from fidgeting. "How's Mattie?" she asked, her voice suddenly faltering.

"She's fine. Tricia had her settled for the night."

There was an awkward silence, and suddenly the companionship they had shared the day before seemed like a distant memory. For one heart-stopping instant they stared at each other, invisibly linked by an acute awareness, then Jase's expression altered dramatically. Looking suddenly very gaunt, he turned away. "I have some paperwork I'd better catch up on," he said gruffly. Susan felt as though he were severing a vital link as she watched him walk away. He had barricaded his feelings behind an unyielding belief, and both of them, unfortunately, were going to have to live with his decision.

Trying to block out the ache that had settled in her chest, she went into the main kitchen and started making apple pies with a vengeance, her mood swings bouncing from righteous anger to absolute misery. But mostly she felt as though all the lightness had been drained from her, leaving behind a leaden heaviness.

It was after ten when she finished cleaning up the kitchen and put the last four pies in the oven, then went for a quick bath. Instead of putting on her regular clothes, she slipped into a brightly colored cotton wrap that her brother had sent her from the Bahamas. It was really a beach cover-up, but it was cool and comfortable, and the kitchen was so unbearably hot after having the oven on for so long.

The phone rang just as she was taking the pies out of the oven, and she itched to answer it, but she knew Jason would. She was sure it was Carol with news about Davy, and she simply could not wait to find out what the specialist had said. She started for the door, then turned back to the cupboard and cut Jason a large wedge of hot pie, topping it with a scoop of ice cream. Pouring a single cup of coffee, she picked up a fork and once again started down the corridor that led past Jason's room.

She found him in the living room, stretched out on the sofa with one arm draped across his eyes, a grim set to his mouth. A single lamp cast the room in heavy shadows and a cool breeze wafted in from the screen door that led onto the veranda.

Her eyes solemn, she quietly set the coffee and dessert down on the coffee table.

He lifted his arm and looked at the large wedge of apple pie then glanced up at her, a touch of humor in his eyes. "What happened to good old chicken soup?"

She smiled and sat down on the corner of the table. "Don't you know anything? You get chicken soup when you have the flu, and you get apple pie and ice cream when you feel like holding your head in the watering trough."

That made him smile, and he hauled himself up and leaned back against the wide arm, then reached for the plate. "Walter will kill me if he finds out I was into his apple pie."

"Who are you kidding? Walter has trouble killing flies." She watched him for a moment, then asked quietly, "What did Carol have to say about Davy?"

He didn't look up, but she sensed that same tight control she'd witnessed at the hospital. "He's okay. The specialist wants him to stay out of the sun for a couple of days and not expose his eyes to any irritants, but there's no damage."

She let out a sigh of relief. "Thank God."

His voice had little strength to it. "Those kids were so damned lucky."

Susan didn't know what to say to ease his mood so she said nothing and watched him eat his pie in silence. When he finished, he slid the empty plate back on the table and, still without looking at her, he finally spoke. "I don't know how to thank you for being there for him today. It could have been such a frightening experience for him if he hadn't had someone with him."

"Don't thank me," she admonished gently. "I went because I wanted to."

He finally looked up at her. "I know that." He gazed at her for a moment then leaned his head back and stared at the ceiling. "You never think about what a big space a kid fills in your life until something threatens him. Then it hits home how very fragile life really is." He rested his arm across his eyes again, and she saw him swallow hard before he continued, his voice strained. "I don't know what I would have done if something had happened to that kid. I really don't know."

Susan slipped over to the sofa and sat down beside him, and with the ache in her throat nearly suffocating her, she gently took his hand in hers and drew his arm down. There was a wealth of understanding and compassion in her eyes as she stroked his taut face. "Don't do that to yourself, Jase. Don't. That kind of thinking is usually motivated by guilt, and you have nothing to feel guilty about."

His hand tightened around hers. "But I do," he said hoarsely. "I came within an inch of rejecting that kid in the most destructive way possible, and it's going to haunt me for the rest of my life."